WE ARE THE WORLD
WE ARE THE CHILDREN

A NOVEL

By Brian Zaca

WE ARE THE WORLD,

WE ARE THE CHILDREN

You Only Live Once series

(YOLO) series

For more information:

http://www.yolo.org.za

Book and Cover design by iWYZe Publishers.

First Edition: January 2019

DEDICATION

The "We Are the World" is a song and charity single recorded by the United Support of Artists (USA) for Africa in 1985. It was written by Michael Jackson and Lionel Richie and produced by Quincy Jones for the album We Are the World. This book is dedicated to every musician who was part of the USA for AFRICA mission. Africa thanks you. I would also love to dedicate the book to the Save the Children organization that still plays a major role in helping our children in Africa today and to everyone who has found their gift, their innate 'treasure,' and purpose and uses it to change the world.

You have a limited time to stay on earth. You must try to use that period for the purpose of transforming your country into what you desire it to be: a democratic, non-racial, non-sexist country. And that is a great task.

_Nelson Mandela

1

1966

Every minute, a child died. In the barren land, the mothers whimpered for their dying children and the babies wailed in the absence of fathers, husbands and sons who were engrossed in war.

Gunshots echoed through the air and the sky was grey with smoke and teargas. The cattle were scrawny, bony and resembled hand sketches drawn by toddlers. The babies' bodies and faces were thinner than thin. They had clearly carved out sharp features of bones poking through their skin, their cheeks were hollowed-in, their hair was yellowish and chunks of it were falling off. The babies didn't play or sing, even six year olds crawled without the strength to walk. The poor babies were always tired and if you got closer to them, all you heard was the growling of their bloated stomachs, their soft cry and you could see their discomfort through their fidgety, bony legs.

Sululta, a countryside in Ethiopia, was like a boat out in the ocean, tossed back and forth by a harrowing raging tempest of poverty, famine, war and disease. The time was gruesome and evil, beyond human thought for the entire country. Ethiopia had no rudder - no direction or control, no edification, except the catastrophe that gripped the country like a baby nursing on its mother.

The national liberation war became worse and raged throughout Eritrea and other parts of Ethiopia. At the break of dawn, soldiers set every grass hut ablaze. They didn't care who was inside the house, they wanted to kill everyone, women and children. The children screamed and yelled, the women wailed, carrying their little ones and scudded out of the houses. Some women were shot with their children in their arms and died at the scene.

The soldiers shot everyone they stumbled upon, especially young men and boys. Those who got away fled through to the bushes. Smoke filled the skies of the early mornings. The smell of burnt dried grass permeated the entire village.

Young children scurried through the woods alone, crying, hungry and some injured. The older children took care of the younger ones and carried them on their backs. Child headed households were a norm. It was children taking care of children. Young children of as little as five years old, had to look out for their younger siblings, provide for them, feed them, bathe them, nurture them and give them hope.

The cry of the children in the dry forest was maudlin and melancholic. They made their way to safety at the Save the Children Feeding Centre. There was not a single adult amongst them, all their mothers were shot or burnt to death. How were these kids going to break free from this bondage?

***

DUST BLEW IN THE AIR as the tyres of Dr Pittman's van scraped the dry, dusty parched road. Her white van had large tyres with deep treads and big blocks. They could trample over any solid rock and scrape out of any mud pile, no matter how deep it was.

Dr Pittman was a very young Medical Doctor, straight out of medical school, who travelled from the United States of America to commit her life to helping sick children in Sululta, Ethiopia. By birth she was British and you never had to ask her what country she was from, her accent always gave her away.

After she did her residency, she dedicated her life to serve in Africa as a local doctor. She was part of a Medical Volunteer Abroad Programme for junior doctors, at an organisation called Save the Children.

In the mornings, Dr Pittman travelled to the Save the Children clinical compound and Feeding Scheme Centre and she followed the same route every day which was chiefly the longest route to the Centre. Her reason for taking the longest route was because she wanted to see if there was any child she could help along the road.

The Centre was comprised of big, white tents, held up by big steel poles and thick ropes. The tents had plastic sheets as windows and within were strings and strings of medical gurneys lined up in rows of fifties and the sick little babies were stacked two kids per bed and sometimes, they would even kick each other off. Day and night the cacophony of crying babies echoed through the tents and the entire place smelt of disinfectant. It was that all familiar smell of a hospital, yet it was a little more melancholic.

During the morning, the outside of the Centre smelt like oat meal porridge, cooked with big silver pots by a cadre of young women called Community Care Givers, their shortened names were CCGs and in the afternoon, the outside of the Centre smelt of vegetable soup. The CCGs were the women responsible for providing basic care to children at the most basic levels. Their duties were to bed wash the babies, feed them, monitor their medicine and make sure the babies received a healthy balanced meal daily.

Dr Pittman's car stereo cracked as she stretched her hand to set it to the correct frequency. The Ethiopian President was on air, "…to say that Ethiopia has no hope," the President said, "is an asinine and dumb statement. Ethiopia has hope and the hope is in our children and youth. If our children will gather together, rise up in their youth and build the fabric of their societies, Ethiopia will rise again. Nevertheless, Ethiopia also needs help from everyone in and outside of our country. Helps us build Africa and help us beat the hallowing effects of war, famine and poverty."

"Humph," Dr Pittman gasped, sneering at the stereo. "It must be the only *sensible* thing you've ever said since you were elected. Maybe it's time they got a woman in there."

She looked outside the window as the mothers waved at her on their way to the Save the Children Centre. She smiled at them with crinkled eyes glittering with tears, waving back them. Every time they saw her, their faces beamed and they yelled, "Dokiteri," repeatedly dancing. They didn't dance because life was giddy sunshine and rainbows, they danced because the presence of one person, always gave them hope. Dr Pittman always made their babies feel a little bit better than the day before or even an hour before that.

Some of the mothers squirmed and fiddled sitting in line on the long, oak benches outside the Centre waiting to see Dr Pittman. The mothers bared in their arms, dying and crying little babies with gloomy, penetrating and melancholy voices that made every mother want to take her own life, or bare the pain for her own child, if only she could. If the child stopped crying, it meant the child died.

The babies' skins were dry and scaly. Their stomachs bloated, teeth decaying, ribs poked vividly through their bodies, yellow mucus dribbling down their noses, drying up like cement from the dusty sand. Their little bodies, that should have been running, flying, jumping, spinning, twisting and turning, *were dying*, crawling on the dusty soil scraping their little knees and elbows.

On one of the benches, alongside the white tents, was a young, unknown mother who sat tapping her feet and fanning her babies face with her hands, her eyes were crinkled in frustration, swollen and glittering with tears. A lump was lodged in her throat and her face was screwed up in a manner that indicated that she would burst into tears at any moment.

The woman was younger and more sentimental than the other mothers. She rocked her legs up and down in rapid movements, whilst her child wailed and whimpered on her lap, fiddling with his little fragile legs. The young mother could not bear the pain in her child's outcry any longer and she was now crying along with her baby. She was only sixteen years old, raped and mutilated by an Ethiopian army and air force soldier nine months before that.

The mother then saw Dr Pittman pulling off at the Centre with her sallying forth, sashaying her hips towards the entrance with brisk and long strides, jangling and fumbling with the keys in her hands, trying to shove them into her handbag. The young mother's eyes turned into owl eyes and she leaped in to action, flew off the bench with fiery tenacity, feet hammering the solid ground and she then stampeded towards Dr Pittman with relentless desperation, pushing her way forward through the long line, whilst brandishing her child in the air, crying out, "Dokiteri, dokiteri, igeza dokiteri." This means 'Doctor, doctor, help me doctor' in Amharic. When she got to Dr Pittman, she shoved the little baby boy into her arms, as if she was carrying a bag of hot coal.

Dr Pittman froze and her eyes blew wide open, her jaw slackened to her chest and she stood there gobsmacked holding the wailing baby in her arms. The young woman whispered something in her ear and fled, weeping and sulking, running as fast as she could, not looking backwards. She kept running and running until she disappeared into the dry woods and never came back, ever again.

When Dr Pittman open the little boy's hands, there was a little note written in Amharic saying:

Widi hābiti

This meant *'Treasure'*, which is the name that Dr Pittman gave the little unknown boy.

Later that night, they found the young woman hanging from the African Juniper tree near the riverbank… she was dead.

A month later, at the apex of the war, Dr Pittman had to return to the USA. She left Treasure in the care of Mrs

Wedu, a small scale gardener who had a penchant for gardening.

Dr Pittman had the little boy wrapped in a blanket. The boy's hair was black again and his body was fuller. She leaned forward over the bundle, "Could I – could I say goodbye to him?" she asked. Mrs Wedu proffered the baby back, smiling. Dr Pittman bent her blond head forward over Treasure. Her hair tumbled over his face and she gave him a very ticklish kiss with her hair on his face. She suddenly let out a sulky croak.

"Don't cry Doctor," Mrs Wedu said. "I'll take good care of him."

"So-s-sorry," Dr Pittman sobbed, taking out a spotted handkerchief and burying her face in it. "I just can't stand it, how will these kids live without me. I-I just can't leave him."

"Shhh!" Mrs Wedu hissed patting Dr Pittman gingerly on her shoulder. "Everything is going to be okay. Maybe not today, but everything will change."

Dr Pittman darted a tearful glance at Mrs Wedu, how can she be so positive, she wondered. The whole of Ethiopia was up in flames, babies are dying every day. She laid Treasure gently back into Mrs Wedu's arms. For a full minute, the two of them stood and looked at the little bundle; Dr Pittman blinked ferociously, her organisation's car was waiting to transport her to the airport. A big bang sound, that sounded like a bomb exploded a distance away.

"Dr Pittman," the driver shouted through the passenger door. "We have to go now."

"Promise me something," Mrs Wedu said. "Promise me you're going to come back and help our kids."

Dr Pittman sulked even more, "I promise," she said, stroking his shoulder.

"Don't worry," Mrs Wedu said. "I will take good care of him, just like you taught me."

Dr Pittman nodded, "Goodbye, Mrs Wedu."

"Good bye, Doctor, you made a difference. Maybe one day, more people like you will come and help us."

Wiping her eyes with her handkerchief, Dr Pittman sniffed, swung her legs on the bar, sunk herself on the seat and they drove off. Just a distance further, Dr Pittman looked through the sideview mirror and watched Mrs Wedu cuddling the little bundle in her arms.

"Good luck, Treasure," Dr Pittman murmured. She looked ahead and they were out of sight.

Treasure rolled in his blanket, not knowing that he was special. The boy didn't know that people all around the country, who were waiting for a saviour, were waiting for him. He was the Treasure of the country. Nobody knew that the child was born with a gift that would change the world.

2

December 1983

The sun fell asleep behind the ocean, shutting its red eyes in the late afternoon and grey clouds gathered in the sky as Professor Pittman stretched her legs and sunk her feet in the crusty sea sand for her everyday one-mile afternoon jog. Her skin was mushy and red, with sweat dripping down her brow and the sour taste in her mouth made her thirst for a sip of water, not to mention her legs were burning. You may think that she hated this, but it made her feel good about herself. The pain was a sign of life to her.

She sprinted the last couple of steps, stretching her legs and her limits, pushing herself as her Ralf cheered her on, looking at the stopwatch in his hands. "C'mon push yourself, you're almost there, almost there… EXCELLENT," shouted Ralf clicking of the stopwatch when Professor Pittman got to the bench. "Well done, well done, super-woman."

Professor Pittman chuckled, panting with her mouth wide open, trying to catch her breath, with her chest inflating and deflating like a balloon.

Ralf lifted the stopwatch in her face, grinning, "Mm, impressive, you hit a new record, a minute and a half early today."

Professor Pittman grunted, rolling her eyes upward, "Dammit," she gasped, with hands rested on her knees, "That's still not good enough."

"Argh rubbish, c'mon," Ralf blurted, nudging her on her shoulders. "Progress not perfection? You're doing great. Don't be so hard on yourself. Remember you're running on sand, you'd be much faster on solid soil. If you seek out perfection, you might die trying to reach it."

Professor Pittman emitted a loud sigh as she dropped herself on the bench, picked up her water bottle and squashed a stream off water down her throat and exhaled out loud, "you should come join me now," she said still breathless.

Ralf chuckled, "What? So you can emasculate me in front of all these people? And make me look like an idiot," he said, deadpan. "When those feet of yours hit the ground you're like a lightning bolt and that's crazy."

There were couple of joggers running past them, the seagulls were whistling up ahead and the ocean cracked against the rocks. The sour smell of the ocean, was like fresh perspiration.

Professor Pittman chuckled, grabbed her gym bag and they walked to Ralf's car. She was flushed, but it was hard to see because her face was already red. "Back in high school," she said. "You used to beat me though. You used to be really good."

Ralf smiled, "Yes, but that was then, now you're just a machine."

Professor Pittman darted a subtle glance at him, "I still can't believe you introduced me to running and then left me running alone like a crazy woman. Men have a real bad habit of leaving women hanging," she said with a mischievous look on her face.

"Well, I couldn't bare the humiliation of being out run by a woman."

Professor Pittman smiled, throwing her gym bags in the car trunk as Ralf moved around to the driver's seat.

He was the only friend she had and she was the only friend he had. But Ralf wanted to be more than friends with her. If there was a woman he wanted to marry, it was Cathy Pittman. Well back then she was only Cathy without her accolades. They became good friends since Professor Pittman's father moved his business from Britain to Washington DC. However, she never had time for love. She was ambitious, driven to follow her dreams, became a doctor and later she fled to Ethiopia after her residency. Even though Ralf tried to forget about her, he never could. He married and later divorced a year later when Professor Pittman returned from Ethiopia in April 1966 and she sometimes questioned whether her return resulted in Ralf divorcing his wife.

After her return to America, she spent her days researching what diseases the children may have had. She advanced herself, did her post-doctoral studies and became a professor at the Massachusetts Institute of Technology and a senior lecturer in paediatric infectious diseases.

Ralf was broad in his forties, with big shoulders, blond hair and blue eyes. He tumbled over Professor Pittman's little stature and she felt safe around him.

The clouds gathered above them in thick grey sheets and tiny drops of rain dropped from the sky. When they got in the car Professor Pittman turned up the car stereo and the reporter announced, "…it seems like the catastrophe in Ethiopia has moved from bad to worse," the reporter said. "…and environmentalists believe that it could get worse and could end up taking more than half a million lives before the end of this year…"

When Professor Pittman heard the news, her body went into an immediate slump and her heart sank, "oh no, not again" she groaned lifting her hand to her forehead. She could still vividly see, in her mind, the images of dying and hungry children, crawling on the cracked and dusty ground like insects, from the first time she was there. She felt a lump lodge in her throat and Ralf could see her countenance becoming morose as she leaned her head against her hand with her elbow on the window seal, watching the raindrops dropping from the heavens.

Knowing the pain it brought her, Ralf switched off the stereo, "you should stop doing that to yourself," he said. "You can't help all those children, Cathy. You did what you could do, you played your role and you should be proud of yourself."

She shook her head, “No Ralf, this time it’s a thousand times worse,” Professor Pittman said, her voice mournful and eyes glistening, as the tears welled up. “You can’t possibly tell me that it’s like when I was there. This is manslaughter.”

“But you can’t do anything about it Cathy, can you?” Ralf said. “It’s a part of nature -”

“No it’s not nature,” Professor Pittman retorted. “Farmers are now suffering from the widespread confiscation of land by the wealthy classes and government of Emperor Haile Selassie.” Exasperation and frustration radiated on her face, as her passion grew. “The wealthy classes and the Ethiopian government are ignoring both the famine and the people who are dying,” she said and sighed and there was a surge of silence. Ralf didn’t want to say anything further with the fear of further annoying her. “You know,” she said, finally. “I always pray that if people could just gather together, rise up and build the fabric of their own societies and if everyone in the world, every American included, could just give something, anything, no matter how small… Africa would be a better place.” She looked out the window, watching kids jump, yell and play in the rain, rolling on the floor in laugher and green coated lawns.

"Kids were meant to be happy, they were meant to laugh and play… not die in pain," she murmured as she thought of the sight of the malnourished kids she left in Sululta.

Professor Pittman believed deep in her gut, that she was supposed to help those children. She could not flee from the memories that lingered, memories and dreams of dying children. She had iron fetters bound against her like a slave on a galley ship. The heart wants what it wants and her heart never could let go of the little boy, her umbilical cord remained connected to him. Treasure was her son.

Dispelling her tempestuous longing heart was not as simple as turning on a light switch. She had no doubt that one day she would return, but she just never knew how she would do it and when. Her heart remained restless. She was at the apex of her career, but something bothered her, something deep, something bubbled within her like a volcano, ready to explode. She wondered why she was unhappy and yet had so much going for her. Winning a noble price didn't do it, starting her own medical private practice didn't do it, dating didn't do it, working harder didn't do it although that's what she did to compensate for her loneliness, working harder.

***

PROFESSOR PITTMAN sat reading on her comfortable plush couch, whilst the fire crackled in the fireplace, the mouth-watering aroma of her coffee shrouded the living room and the turkey roasted golden in the oven as the snowflakes drizzled outside, coating the grass and mountains white. She had a very comfortable house with panelled walls, tiled floors with sections of carpets, thickly cushioned couches and numerous books circling the walls of the living room in which she sat for hours and hours, reading until she passed out.

In the background, in a soft melody, she was playing her favourite song, 'Do they know it's Christmas?'

'…But say a prayer, Pray for the other ones

At Christmastime it's hard, but when you're having fun

There's a world outside your window

And it's a world of dread and fear

Where the only water flowing

Is the bitter sting of tears

And the Christmas bells that ring there are the clanging chimes of doom

Well tonight thank God it's them instead of you

And there won't be snow in Africa this Christmastime

The greatest gift they'll get this year is life

Where nothing ever grows

No rain nor rivers flow

Do they know it's Christmastime at all?

Here's to you

Raise a glass for everyone

Spare a thought this yuletide for the deprived

If the table was turned would you survive

Here's to them

Underneath that burning sun

You ain't gotta feel guilt just selfless

Give a little help to the helpless

Do they know it's Christmastime at all?

Feed the world

Feed the world

Let them know it's Christmastime again...'

She shared the song with many of her friends and colleagues at work, but they just didn't get why she did it, because everyone knew the song already, but she still did it anyway. It never had the same effect on them as it had on her. The song had so much meaning, so much heart, so much sense and so much purpose. She couldn't reason how anyone could not feel what she felt when she listened to it. She always said the same thing to them whenever she bestowed the song upon them, "this might help you change the world," she would say.

She could see her colleagues were getting sick of it, sometimes they'd mock her about it and every year someone would gift her with the same song.

Professor Pittman had the book laying open on her chest as she fell asleep on her couch and the dream came back again. "Widi hābiti," the young woman said in the dream. The young woman was Treasure's mother. The dream persisted like a dripping tap. *Widi hābiti*, the woman's words echoed in her mind. Alas, the dream was a bit different that day - the young mother was telling her a story and the last words of that story she could remember were "*Tenesuna tegenibu*".

She woke up in a flinch, when a strong wind blew against the open window in the kitchen, in a heart-jolting bang. She leapt up from her sleep, sweaty and panting as if rising from the dead. The last words of the story beamed at her like a beacon. These words mean "Rise up and Build" in Amharic.

Right then and there she knew…

It was time to heed the call.

***

THE NEXT DAY, whilst Professor Pittman was cleaning the weeds in her food garden, Ralf pulled off at her house, "I see you're doing very good work with your garden," Ralf said. "It's a great skill you have."

Professor Pittman chuckled, "If only I could take the credit for it," she said. "Mrs Wedu taught me this, god she was so talented in it. It's like she had magic."

Ralf laughed, "I'm sure she was, because you talk about her a lot."

Professor Pittman shook her head, "you know," she said. "I still don't know how that woman did it. It's like everything around her disappeared when she was working in her garden and in mine too." Every time Professor Pittman talked about Mrs Wedu, she spoke about her with so much passion and admiration. She continued, "Gardening and planting vegetables was such a big thing to her, whilst everyone was unhappy, depressed sad and struggling. This woman was so confident, so peaceful, so hopeful and so full of happiness. She was so connected to her inner self, independent from other people's opinions. The status, the rewards, the popularity, the prestige were less important to her. She had a different sense of courage and faith – she had so much purpose, yet all she did was - plant vegetables."

Ralph smiled, "The most valuable result of all education is the ability to do the thing you have to do when it needs to be done," he said. "People who love painting must paint, novelists must write and gardeners must plant, if they want to be at peace with themselves and their surroundings. Every living person must be true to their own nature and purpose. What a person can be, they must be... It's called self-fulfilment, the tendency of a person becoming what they're called to be... even if their purpose is gardening... If you do the thing you want to do the most, living becomes less painful and more purposeful." Ralph said, gazing at Professor Pittman deep in her eyes and she stared back at him with owl eyes glittering with tears. "And I guess that's why you called me to come here?" Ralph continued. "You're going back to Ethiopia isn't it?"

3

1984

It was all in the news all over the world.

Bob Geldof was an Irish singer-songwriter and political activist. He was a very ordinary man, but also not that ordinary. A man who grew up in an ordinary part of Dublin. Bob, accompanied by his friend, James 'Midge' Ure, a Scottish musician, travelled to Ethiopia, to witness the catastrophe first hand.

The sun streamed through the vehicle windows, yet his mind was foggy when he saw calamity. They settled in a village called Sululta and they visited Tewahedo Christian High School. The cows, camels, sheep and goats looked as though the hot wind would blow them away like withered leaves.

On their way to the school, tears welled up in their eyes. The sight of scrawny babies crawling on the ground and dead cattle was unbearable. There was a cattle laying on its side, eyes opened, its mouth gaped slightly open and a purple tongue hung out. Flies buzzed around the corpse and a swarm of insects covered the whole body.

"Genocide," Midge Ure said, looking out of the van windows. "This is what this is. This is not famine. Something that causes more murders and pain than the human mind can take… genocide."

A year had passed since Professor Pittman returned to Sululta. She was the one transporting them with the vehicle from her organisation. The van was white, with a big wheel and had Save the Children written in red on the side of the door.

"This is just a part of it," Professor Pittman said. "I've seen little babies eaten alive by vultures."

Bob Geldof glanced at her through the rear-view mirror and swallowed. The road was quite bumpy as well as dry and they shook as if they were on a Disney Land ride. Bob felt a lump lodge in his throat and the tears flowed unabated down his cheeks. Men don't cry, but imagining that this could have been his daughter or son crawling on the ground, with vultures soaring ravenously above, made his spine tremble.

"Every minute," Professor Pittman said in a low tone. "THREE children die of starvation, a mother kills herself from depression, or a father dies of Aids. No matter how hard we try, we just can't save them all."

When Professor Pittman moved back to Sululta, she volunteered to teach Biology at the local high school, a tattered school made of strong mud bricks, where more than 200 grade twelve learners were squashed into one room. They sat in long rows and desks like a jury panel in court. The entire class shared three biology books that Professor Pittman bought them. The kids were gaunt and faint.

All the scholars thought that Professor Pittman's British accent was amusing. She had a pointy nose and thin lips, average height, with the small stature of an athlete and she loved running. She conducted herself as though she was in her late sixties, filled with wisdom and rich experiences, unique insights and inspiring concepts. Her blond hair glowed and she had green eyes. Her smile was galactic and she wore youthful clothes that didn't expose much of her body.

In the early hours of the mornings, she worked as a paediatrician at the local clinic, during certain periods, she volunteered at Tewahedo Christian High School, a school built by the Ethiopian Orthodox Tewahedo

Church, teaching Biology and during the late hours of the afternoon, she took care of children at her compartment. This was outside her work.

They climbed out of the vehicle and the kids who had the energy, danced and laughed because Professor Pittman had told them that Bob Geldof was a very famous man, who was going to sing them a song. The scholars beamed even in the midst of immense poverty.

Bob Geldof hugged and kissed the children, holding his guitar in his other hand. How could they be so happy? Still children, their look of innocence made their stomachs congeal in sadness, as the heavy burdens appeared, written all over their little fragile bony bodies. When they picked up a child, they felt as if they were holding a hamster in their hands, they felt the rips and sometimes heard the bloated stomachs growl.

Bob Geldof and Midge Ure looked at each other. They were speaking but without words. How in the living God do people survive in this condition?

Bob held a little girl in his arms, after Professor Pittman introduced them and gave a special word for them. The little girl's face was thinner than thin, clearly carving out her sharp features, leaving the attention not on her full, cracked lips, not on her sucked-in cheeks, but on her tired eyes. She would die at any minute.

Bob tried to say some encouraging words of hope to the scholars, but he couldn't. What was he to say to them? Back home he had a fridge full of food, a warm bed, green grass, running water, a hot tub, a warm bed, spoiled kids, Christmas was around the corner, but do they even know that Christmas is coming. There was absolutely nothing to say, all they could do is sing the children a song. Maybe it won't stop the hunger, but for a moment, just for a moment, it will let them forget about the pain.

Bob began finger picking on his guitar and they sang the song, 'Do they Know It's Christmas. Heartfelt and maudlin, neither could hold their tears back.

Soon, it was time for them to leave. They waved through opened windows. Treasure pushed past the crowd with force, "Mr Geldof, Mr Geldof," he shouted repeatedly.

Bob peered at Treasure and the look on Treasure's eyes, said something to him, "Stop the car, stop the car," Bob shouted at Professor Pittman.

The car stopped abruptly, "What is it son?"

Treasure was panting, "T-Thank you, for visiting our school," he said, stammering.

Bob nodded, "It's our pleasure… sorry what's your name."

"Treasure, my name is Treasure Wedu."

Bob stuck out his hand, "Nice to meet you Treasure," he said smiling.

"You're American," Treasure asked, "like Professor Pittman?"

Bob chuckled, "No, no I'm Irish, I was born in Ireland… but Michael Jackson… he's an American."

Midge and Professor Pittman had their backs turned, looking behind them.

Treasure nodded, "The Americans, will they come to help us… will they come and save the children from dying, like Professor Pittman? And what about Michael Jackson, Lionel Richie and Quincy Jones, will they come and help us like you…?"

Bob stared at Treasure with a smirk, and his heart was pumping custard, yet he felt his eyes get watery. All these kids needs is hope, he thought. He gulped, "Well, I don't know son… but I can promise you one thing… I will come and help you."

Treasure beamed with a broad smile, "T-Thank you, Mr Geldof, bring the kids some toys too."

Bob, Midge and Professor Pittman chuckled, "We will," Bob said. "We will, take care of yourself and remember, you too can save the children."

Treasure's eyes popped open, "How? How can I save them?"

Bob brooded, "One gift, it always takes one gift to change the world… A little help can go a long way. We all have a purpose and a gift within us… just as your name says, Treasure. We all have a Treasure within us and around us. Which is our purpose and we need to help others fulfil their purpose… so we are ALL Treasure Hunters… so make a difference and use your Treasure."

Treasure brooded for a moment, making sense of it, "I have one," Treasure blurted out. "A talent… I-"

Bob raised his hand, "No," he retorted cutting Treasure short. "You don't need to tell me what it is. The gift is yours. It is your valued possession, your treasure.

Now all you have to do is to use it and help someone. Leave your mark my boy."

Treasure starred as the car drove away. The words had hit straight to his heart. They were somewhat comforting as well. It was not the first time he heard something like that. Professor Pittman always spoke about purpose, but it really didn't make any sense. But can he really change the world with his gift? Was his gift big enough? All he had, was the gift of kindness and generosity? But how could he use that?

"He's one of them," Professor Pittman said as the car disappeared from the scholars. "When he was little, his mother left him in my arms; he was a very sick baby. I took him under my care, but I had to leave him with someone, because it was time for me to leave."

"Where was his mother?" Bob asked.

Professor Pittman glanced at Bob through the rear-view mirror, "She killed herself," she said. "Hanged herself from a tree. He's so smart and he remembers everything you tell him… so you must keep your promise, otherwise… it's going to destroy him."

Bob was moved by the plight of starving children in Ethiopia and he felt an idea bubbling in his mind, perhaps to put into practice what he had just told the boy. He nodded, "I'll come back… I have a plan and it might just work."

4

The next day, Treasure sat in his classroom as Professor Pittman droned on in biology class, whilst gazing through the window looking at the matured cracks, dredged deep down the barren, parched soil like a wizened old face, roasted hard, showing no more benevolence to the seeds that were scattered on it. The region was wan and dry, unfertilised and dehumanised, not brown, grey or beige, only the colour of death that covered the entire region.

Being hungry was a part their lives. An adequate diet was a luxury for the rich. Their stomachs stayed empty from sun up until sundown. The only rule was; you did not ask where anything came from; you just ate what you got. If nobody knew, nobody could tell. Livestock died and there were was no earthworms to fish with and the rivers were drying up, streaming down at ankle high levels. The whole Sululta region was waiting, but they did not know what they were waiting for.

She shared a story of Rosa Parks and the scholars perched on their chairs, peering at her attentively, sitting as still as sleeping owls on branches. Their attention never drifted or wandered away, nor did their heads jerk from sleepiness. They were utterly stiff necked.

Her enthusiasm bubbled as she told her students the Rosa Parks story, "…the white man tried with all means to intimidate Mrs Parks…" Professor Pittman said. "And during those days, it was the law that said black people were to give up their seats for any white person. Mrs Rosa Parks was bold, courageous, tenacious and bodacious. She refused to surrender her seat to a white passenger on a segregated Montgomery bus, which spurred on the 381-day Montgomery Bus Boycott that helped launch nationwide efforts to end segregation of public facilities," Professor Pittman said using fierce gestures filled with gusto, clenching her fists tighter.

She paused with a diligent scan through the scholars' countenances. She had their attention and continued, "they arrested Mrs Parks that day and she became an example that prompted an influential civil rights demonstration in Montgomery," she said. "… Mrs Parks' story changed the world… she had dedicated her life, to her purpose." That was what she loved talking about – Purpose and Destiny.

The students gazed at her without blinking, their eyes fixed with inspiration as they sat as quiet as mice while she told them the story, slowly manoeuvring herself backwards through the rows of the desks, towards the black board. "You only live once," Professor Pittman said lifting her index finger. "Only once and if you had the chance to change the world today, would you do it? What are the things that you would do if you knew you couldn't fail?

Her voice dwindled as the saliva gathered in her throat, her heart ached with sadness as though she contemplated a sad part of her own life. She cleared her throat and raised her posture hiding her half-trembling hands behind her back, "by the time, people reach a mature age," she said, "or sitting on their deathbed, past their prime, they begin to look back at the plans they made and the dreams they had, things they didn't do, pursue or say and that which never materialised. They are left with regrets of things they did not do and their dreams keep shouting at them, screaming and choking them to death," she said, with her hand clenching her neck.

She continued, "They meander and stroll through life, delaying and decaying every single day and later in life, the longer they wait, the more intense the suffering becomes because guilt is an albatross around their necks," she said, speaking in a manner that indicated that her utterances come from her own experience. "They always say, I'm gonna do it tomorrow and that tomorrow turns into years, years into decades and sooner it becomes never... Sometimes I feel like telling them, 'Yesterday, you said tomorrow, so just do it, you only live once. Leap and strive towards it." She glanced at Treasure and said, "You can change the world with your gift and talents. Your gift, is your Treasure."

The class giggled, because she always looked at Treasure when she said this.

"Everyone in here," she said, "has a gift, talent or passion. That is your Treasure and you need to find it", she chuckled. "So basically all of you are treasure hunters... Your gift will make way for you and push you towards your purpose."

Lucky raised his hand.

"Yes, Lucky?" Professor Pittman said beaming up. She loved it when they asked her questions.

"What's your purpose and how do you find it?"

Professor Pittman lifted her hand to her mouth and looked down, "Mm, good question, what is your purpose and how do you find it?" she repeated putting her hands behind her back and looked out the classroom window in a dreamy state.

She looked intently at a group of kids outside who were sitting on the grass, weary and not playing. Which was abnormal for kids their age. Their cheeks were sucked in and their facial bones stood out. "To have a purpose," she started, "means you know the reason for your existence. In other words, you have descriptively defined why you exist and every day of your life, you make it your mission to fulfil that purpose."

The class was gravely quiet, with only the shallow breathing of her students.

"At your birth a seed is planted," she said. "That seed is your uniqueness. It wants to grow, transform itself and flower to its full potential. It has a natural, assertive energy to it. Your Life's Task is to bring that seed to flower, to express your uniqueness through your work. You have a destiny to fulfil. The stronger you feel and maintain it – as a force, a voice or in whatever form – the greater your chance for fulfilling this Life's Task and achieving mastery.

"Basically, we're on a journey?" Treasure interposed. "A sort of pilgrimage?

Professor Pittman nodded, "That's right," she said. "A pilgrimage that only you can take and no one else but you. Your life purpose is like your fingerprints. Everyone has fingers, but the fine details on the fingers are unique."

Pittman began walking towards the window with her hands clenched behind her back, "When you die," she said in a soft tone, "because we all will one day, I hope that you would not have a single bit of talent, gift or treasure left inside of you. Leave this earth empty… live each day as if it was your last day… moreover Young King and Queen, the question remains." She paused looking outside the window at the sick little babies whilst the group of Community Caregivers outside fed them. She gulped every time she looked at those kids and with sorrow in her heart and a muffled voice, she said, "What can you do to leave the world a better place…? How can you leave your mark in the world…? How can you make a different…? How will the people know that you were here…? And how will you live this one life that you have been gifted with? Because you only get one shot at life to live it right, only one…"

The bell rang and the whole class echoed a long *drawl* disappointed at the bell that had rained on their parade. They loved her stories, they marvelled at her wisdom and council.

"Argh," Professor Pittman gasped checking her watch. "Saved by the bell, uh?"

The whole class reverberated and drawled a long, "Ah."

She chuckled, "You can go and research the Rosa Parks story yourselves and write me a report about your thoughts and remember what I always tell you Young Kings and Queens…" she said, raising her voice higher.

The class amassed and echoed her dictum in unison, "You only live once, but if you do it right, once is enough!"

She pumped her fist in the air, "That's right," she blurted. "You will never bring change when you're already in the cemetery and remember that until the end of your lives Young Kings and Queens and remember, *you can't change and clean up the world if you can't change yourself and clean up your room…*" This statement became the biggest joke in the school because the scholars thought there was nothing important about cleaning their room.

The only people who practised this were Simone and Treasure. Professor Pittman trailed off giving her class homework instructions for the weekend, trying hard to raise her voice above the hubbub and cacophony of screeching chairs, desks and the merry giggling and laughter of students, bubbling with weekend excitement.

After dismissing the class, Professor Pittman summoned Treasure and Simone to remain behind. The two waited for the class to clear and moved closer to Professor Pittman's desk with their bags on their shoulders. They wondered why Professor Pittman had asked them to stay behind. Did they do something wrong? Did they flunk the test? She usually called Treasure for a number of reasons, but why did she call Simone as well?

Simone was the taciturn of the class, she was Professor Pittman's brightest spark and Treasure was her parallel. They had a lot in common and they were her best runners too.

When they had moved closer to her, Professor Pittman stooped down at her desk, pulled out a wrapped package with blue and green wrapping paper, with

'Happy Birthday, Treasure' written on it and proffered it to him, "Happy Birthday, Young King," she said.

Treasure fumbled with the gift in his hands, with a scowl on his forehead, peered at the package in a prolonged squint. No one, ever, in his entire life, had given him a gift. Who would? He had no real friends, his sister hated him, his father was a drunk, his mother sometimes forgot his own birthday and even if she didn't, she had nothing to give. Yet here it was, a huge gift addressed personally to him.

To: Mr Abraham 'Treasure' Wedu

Born: 5th April 1966

Happy Birthday, Young King

Professor Pittman chuckled and patted his shoulder, "Don't worry," she said, grinning. "I also can't believe it's me who wrapped it. It was never my penchant back in High School."

Treasure beamed, all his teeth jutting, his hands were trembling and his heart racing, "T-Thank you, Professor," he said in a placid manner, stammering and unable to take his gleeful and curious gaze off the package.

Professor Pittman smiled, with her head cocked to one side, "It's not every day that a young man turns eighteen, uh…" She always peered at Treasure as though he was some kind of precious pearl, a treasure as his name indicated, or some kind of King. "Now, I have an external task for you two," she said, stretched her hand to the table and proffered a written stack of papers to both of them. "I want you to go home and read this during the weekend… I would like to call that a very special story. I want you to read it and think critically about it and tell me what you've learnt, alright…?"

The two youngsters assented simultaneously, fiddling and perusing through the paper with scowls of confusion and curiosity. Treasure fumbled, unable to grasp the papers simultaneously with the heavy box clenched against his body.

"There's an important message in the story," Professor Pittman said. "And I want you to figure out what it is and oh," she said and chuckled, "please, don't tell me it's a love story."

The two young ones giggled and heeded the task. "Now go on now," she said beckoning them to leave. "Go get to work and get nuts this weekend… "

They assented and started walking towards the door.

"And Oh, Treasure…?" she summoned him before they walked out the door.

Treasure turned around, "Yes, Professor?"

"I'd warn you not to have too much fun," she said beckoning at the box with her eyes. "You still have grade twelve to pass," she winked, "don't dance too much either."

Treasure chuckled, "I won't Professor." They walked out of the classroom and Treasure wondered what the Professor meant when she told him not to dance too much. What was in big box? It could not be a cassette, it's too big?

Stories and novels infatuated Simone. She always walked around school or sat beneath a tree with her eyes glued to a novel or poem that Professor Pittman gave her and if she didn't have one, her gaze was stuck on her feet. She always wore one grey cardigan, a floral skirt and walked with her arms wrapped around her body as though she was feeling cold.

Treasure was not very different from her. He was always in a haste, either running or walking with long strides, reading something, anything he could get his hands on, not paying any attention to anything happening around him. However, his body stature was always fearless and confident. He always combed and patted his hair equally as though he had a black sponge gummed to his head. He was a handsome dark-skinned boy.

Even though Treasure and Simone were in the same class, they never spoke to one another. Nevertheless, something unique set them apart from the rest of the scholars. On his way home, Treasure kept turning the gift around in his hands in awe, with a wide gape dropped to his chest. The package was heavy and it felt expensive. The excitement bubbled inside of him and he couldn't wait to get home. His strides were even longer and sterner and he shook the box next to his ear at times, while walking down the dusty roads.

***

THE STORY HAD BEEN LYING untouched on Treasure's tattered oak bedside table, screaming at him to be read. Everything in his room was old and tattered. But regardless of that, he had an unsullied disposition that gave his room a glow even though there was not much in it. It was a skewed bed, wrapped in blankets that had holes bitten through by rats. He had a bedside table, a wardrobe made out of cardboard and wire and his floor was always smoothly smeared green with cow dung.

Bubbling with curiosity, Treasure was lying prostrate on his bed, whilst twisting and turning his new video camera, pressing buttons and flinching from every spontaneous reaction he got and at times, he would think he had broken something when he didn't get the response he expected. Professor Pittman presented Treasure with a stack of books, a brand new Betamovie BMC-100P camcorder and a battery operated radio. On top of the books, she left a note saying, '*Find your own truth, listen to the song, read the story and think Young King.*'

Treasure teemed with excitement and curiosity; he was exhilarated, "Wow a new camera? And radio?" he said. His grin spread across his face from ear to ear, showing all his perfect, sparkling white piano teeth. He powered the battery operated radio, pressed play on the cassette injected inside and danced to the song playing -

"Do they Know It's Christmas," sung by Bob Gedolf and Midge Ure.

The song reverberated to him with a sacred sense of purpose. Now he knew exactly what Professor Pittman meant when she winked at him and said, 'Don't dance too much,' the song made him dance and made his heart a little giddy. It was love at first hearing and indeed, it was the first song he ever played on his very first gift.

Treasure's guardian mother, whom he only knew as his biological mother, was ploughing the vapid soil in the backyard. The *shing* of the hand trowel dredging into the dry and crusty soil and the *psshh* of the dirt hitting the ground as she dug, hissed a melancholic song of destitution. Sometimes a lonely bird would chirp up high in the branchy trees, sometimes a scrawny cow would moo down at the dry river or his mother would gag from a dry cough or his stomach would growl from its core.

A toppling of morbid nocturnal events terrorised the entire Sululta region; drought, an outbreak of political wars, livestock theft, livestock death, poor agricultural production and it was a catastrophe for the children and their mothers. Their breasts couldn't produce enough milk and they were hanging saggy and wrinkled. Poverty had come home to roost.

The hunger made Treasure squirm and fiddle with his legs, but at least the new video camera and the books scattered on the bed, took his mind off the degrading circumstances around him, even if it was just for a moment. The thought of not knowing where the next meal would come from and living on an empty stomach for two days, would have been an unbelievable story to someone who didn't live in the same country; even Professor Pittman herself could, vicariously, see the pain and hunger. It was ubiquitous. It was obvious - nothing lived in the area.

The other people in the region were poor, but Treasure's family was poorer, the others lacked, but his family lacked even more. It kept him oddly distrait at school and at home.

Treasure stretched his arm over to his bedside table and picked up the stack of papers that contained the sacred story that Professor Pittman vouchsafed him and he began to peruse through it, leaf by leaf. What could be so important about the story? And Simone? Why did Professor Pittman give the story to Simone too? I barely talk to that weird girl.

Treasure started reading aloud as though he was reading a story to a group of kids in a nursery school, bringing the paper closer to his face and almost touching his nose, he wallowed:

'ONCE UPON A TIME, A Young King and Queen found themselves stuck on an island when a strong tempest, with towering, raging waves and strong winds, shipwrecked them left them ashore.

The Young King and Queen spent many days on the island waiting for someone to come and rescue them. They waited as if they were waiting for a Messiah to come. They waited, waited and waited but there was nothing. Every day they woke up and went to the shore of the ocean and gazed over at the horizon and waited. The sun came up and the sun went down as they waited for help to come, but there was nothing. The island was ghostly quiet. There was no ship with cracking and flapping sails, no flares in the sky, nothing, only the whispering of the ocean and the splashing of the waves against the rocks when they ebbed and flowed.

Their eyes narrowed, their breathing grew shallower and any spontaneous, loud sound made them jump abruptly, their eyes would pop open and their hearts would jolt convulsively. They were trembling. They kept glancing at each other when the other wasn't looking. Sometimes their gaze met, but they turned their heads abruptly. They feared each other because they knew not of each other. They were two strangers stuck on an unknown Island.

The sea breeze was like cold needles, pressing on and through their skins. The Young King's teeth were clattering, his body rattling and shaking as the ice-cold wind sank into his bones, leaving his ears stiff and frozen. Rubbing his hands together and blowing some warm breath into them wasn't working either. His nose was as cold as the nose of a seal slithering on ice.

The Young Queen could not pay any attention to the cold breeze. Her stomach was thundering and growling, she was only a little Queen and girls get very hungry. She felt as if there was a hole dredged into her stomach. She was more than famished, more than starving, definitely more than hungry.

Her hunger grew fiercer for the Young Queen was used to being fed grapes and indulging in whatever delicious meals she wanted. She fantasised about food like a man ogling at a beautiful woman. The cold breeze worsened for the Young King who was used to thick and fluffy cloaks. It was becoming colder and colder as the hours sank deeper into the abyss of the afternoon.

The Young King was at his wits end. The cold was unbearable and had a firm grip on him, making him stiff and he was trembling. He had to do something. He rose and gathered some wood to start a fire. The Young Queen could not grant hunger the honour of taking her royal and precious soul. She rose and stepped out into the woods, feigning bravado and confidence, looking for anything she could sink her teeth into.

They both toiled until darkness shrouded them. The Young King gathered as much wood as he could and the Young Queen tried to hunt for as much meat as she could. Their efforts were in vain.

The Young Queen kicked her hunting sticks and stones on the ground, grunting in anger, until the veins in her forehead popped out. She threw herself on the sand, sank her face in her arms and wept. Simultaneously, the Young King kicked the gathered wood, it scattered on the sand, he grunted in anger, his jaw clenched and his knuckles turned white. He sank himself on the sand and hung his raised knees, breathing heavily, his face frozen and tight.

The Young King and Queen sat at the shore of the ocean and still waited. They were still hoping for someone to come and save them. Both of them sat with their knees raised, gazing out into the horizon as the sun shut her eyes behind the sea, as if the ocean itself was a steep mountain to climb.

The Young King was brave. He stood up, shivering, wrapped his arms around himself and walked towards the Young Queen. "I saw you trying to hunt for a deer today" said the Young Kin. He wasn't smiling or smirking, his countenance was fixed. The Queen jumped and leapt onto her feet, wide eyed and her heart pounding. "The quail was right in front of you, but you missed it." He grimaced, disappointed and exasperated. "What kind of useless woman are you?"

The Young Queen felt her heart pounding in her chest, pestered and her emotions were a roller-coaster, her jaw clenched and her beautiful eyes sprang into a vicious, viper-like scowl. "Oh yeah!" the Young Queen sneered in a flippant manner. "You talk about my failures, but look at you. If you had spun, the spindle a couple of more times and faster maintaining pressure, the spindle tip would have begun glowing red and an ember would have formed. Deposit the ember onto the bark, transfer it to a tinder bundle and blow it to become a flame. You're also good for nothing."

The two quarrelled and argued, blurting vicious scoffs and hyperboles at one another, "What kind of man are you?" the Young Queen exclaimed, "you're a good for nothing knuckle head. You're a failure," she shouted. "What kind of man fails to prepare a fire?"

The Young King's blood boiled, "No," he shoved his finger in her face, "you're the failure because you can't even catch a lousy, feeble quail."

They argued and argued and began to wrestle each other. One over the other, they rolled on the rough sand, until they were worn out and lay beside each other, panting and out of breath. They had squandered all their energy. Now, they were both ravenous and cold.

"What's your name?" the Young King growled, without a smile or smirk. His voice stern, deep, brusque and bold.

The Young Queen glanced at him with an air of arrogance and pride, "Why do you ask for my name? Why don't you give me yours?"

"I asked you first!" the Young King said. "You ought to give me your name first. Didn't your mother teach you manners? You don't answer a question with a question, young lady!"

The Young Queen was haughty, she leapt up onto her feet and sneered, "Young Lady? Who are you calling young lady, you pompous air head? You know what, I don't know you

Mister and I would be out of my wits to give you my name? Didn't your mother teach you not to talk to strangers?"

Once again, they quarrelled and argued until nearing darkness, the Young King said, "Okay listen, let's come up with a solution. I can see the goose bumps on your skin and your stomach is rumbling like thunder."

The Young Queen wrapped her arms around her stomach embarrassed.

"And you can see me shiver," the Young King said. "Why don't we huddle up together to keep warm and tomorrow, we rise and build a home we can sleep in, so both of us would be warm until help comes? We will die in this cold."

The Young Queen thought about it and she deemed it a brilliant idea. The Young Queen nodded, "Okay, but it doesn't mean I like you or we are friends."

The Young King stuck out his hand, "Deal," and they shook hands. "Signed, sealed and delivered… I'll sleep at the back," he said, with a mischievous grin.

Her eyes popped open. "And why do you want to sleep behind me? Don't you dare get any silly ideas Mister?" she said, pointing a finger at him.

The Young King chuckled, "Listen, it's too cold for that and I'm too tired. If we don't do this we will die. And besides, I have more muscle then you." He flexed a bicep and she smiled, "I'll keep you warmer," he said.

The Young Queen brooded and they sunk to the cold sand, sleeping one behind the other. He wrapped his arms around her and threw his legs over her. She winced in this comfort and whimpered. They held each other like lovers, though they were not. After a few minutes of lying down, the Young Queen felt something hard poking her on her back. "What do you have hidden in your pants?" she asked. "It's poking me on my back. It's poking, like a cucumber."

The Young King, winced in embarrassment and stammered, "Err, i-it's a stick," he said. "…To protect us from the wild beasts."

The Young Queen had a look of disbelief, "Well, get it out! I won't be able to sleep with it poking my back. Quiet a short stick you use on a wild beast, don't you think?"

"It does get bigger you know," said the Young King. "When it's cold, it shrinks."

"Huh? What kind of stick is that?"

He smiled mischievously, "A royal one."

They slept and soon it was morning. The Young Queen had a peaceful sleep and experienced great dreams. In the morning, they were facing each other, intertwined in each other's arms, like doves. Holding each other tight, with beaming expressions in their sleep, as if they were long time lovers.

The birds were singing a sweet melody, the ocean whistled a lullaby and the breeze massaged their skin. The sun penetrated their eyes, blinding them. It was a beautiful morning. When they opened their eyes and saw themselves facing one another, wrapped in each other's arms, they both leapt onto their feet as if a snake had slithered between them.

The Queen gulped, her cheeks became red and she couldn't keep eye contact. They both could not look at each other. She tucked her hair behind her ears, "S-Sorry," she stammered, downcast.

The Young King chuckled, "So do we begin our building?"

"Err, yeah sure," she said.

"And how was your sleep?" he asked.

She gasped, "I wouldn't bear another night like last night. It was the worst I ever had." She lied, pretending to be absent.

The Young King smirked, with a sideways glance, "Oh yeah? Well, I'm sure I heard you snoring and talking in your sleep."

Her eyes popped open, "Talking in my sleep…? And what was I saying?"

He had a mischievous gleam on his countenance, pursed his lips and shrugged, "Mmm…"

"Perhaps I was talking to the wild beast you wanted to kill with the little stick you had stuck in your pants," she said, gesturing at his groin with her head. "So Mister, little stick man, where do we start?" She was oozing with sarcasm.

He chuckled and then blushed. He became more compassionate and less arrogant. "Well, first we need to know what we have available on the island to construct our house."

She nodded, "When I went hunting, I saw some dried, old deer skin at the other end." She gestured in the direction.

"Excellent we can use it for walls," said the Young King. "When I went gathering for wood to start the fire, I saw some

dried old logs right behind that hill." He pointed in the direction where he had seen the dried wood. "So, excellent, we can cut the deer skin in half and sleep on them and cover ourselves with what remains at night."

The Young King brooded, "Now that we've got all we require for our house, we need a plan on how to build it. I don't know how, my father worked in a butchery and I'm a hunter. I'm good with animals. I'm a King, who came looking for a long lost treasure on the island, but the raging waves tore the ship apart and my servants died in the shipwreck and I survived. I'm a treasure hunter."

The Queen's eyes popped open, "My father was a carpenter and he taught me how to work with wood and skilled me to work with my hands. I can carve anything and build anything using wood. I am a Queen. I too, came looking for the lost treasure on the island, but my servants died in the shipwreck and I survived. I'm a treasure hunter too."

They were getting to know each other. Both were royalty, from whence they came. They had things in common and similar interests. They wanted treasure and understood what treasure was. They both had gifts and the island had valuable resources that they could use to build their house.

The Young Queen thought it was a great opportunity to work together and meet all their needs equally, "Why don't you go and hunt for some food for us and I will gather the wood and build the house for us?" she said.

The Young King agreed, he bowed, curtsying "At your word, your highness." They both smiled at each other and pursued their duties.

The Young King hunted and killed a fat deer and they had more than enough to eat for the day, leftovers for the night and the next day. Their stomachs were as puffed out as a pregnant elephant. They lay inside their little royal abode, their manifestation. Each had their own corner and each had their own view of the beautiful sky. There was more than enough room. It was a warm, cuddly and cozy abode. The Young Queen made the Young King feel like he was in his palace.

The Young Queen laughed, "My stomach is so full, I don't even think I'll be able to sleep. You did a great job, I thought I was gonna die on this island. Now, I have hope."

He chuckled, "Likewise. This place is so warm, I know I'm gonna have a wonderful sleep tonight. You did a great job indeed, Young Queen."

She felt her heart flutter when he called her a Queen. It opened the gates of her soul, she could feel herself blossom and morph into someone different. She gained back her confidence and esteem and so did he. They laughed and tarried looking at the sky, playing and when their hands touched, it was electrifying like lightning striking. Both became lost in the beauty of the stars and the luminous energy of their royal presence made them feel safe around one another. They trusted one another.

The Young King glanced at her, "You know what," he said, "I think I've found me something more than the treasure I was looking for."

The Young Queen, turned her head abruptly and faced him, smiling broadly, "Oh yeah and what would that be, Oh Royal King?"

The Young King smiled, "I've found a friend, someone I can trust and someone I can count on to build a boat to take us back home. Someone with treasure inside of them."

The Young Queen smiled back and blushed, "Yes, you're right," her eyes beamed, "and I've found someone who can help me stay alive for as long as I can. The treasure is inside of us and around us, both of us," she said. "Tomorrow, tomorrow we will rise and build our boat and go back home."

The Young King grinned and said, "Yesterday we said tomorrow, let's rise up and build."

To be continued.....

At the bottom of the story, Professor Pittman wrote a quote by Mahatma Gandhi, *'Be the change that you wish to see in the world.'*

***

After reading the story, Treasure leapt off his bed with a beam on his countenance and stood in front of the mirror brooding, wearing his thinking hat, stroking his chin. What does Professor Pittman want him to learn from the story? Perhaps that circumstance does not make a person, he thought. They push him to identify and discover hidden treasure, gifts and talents that lie within and around him, he wondered. On the other hand, it may mean: *things begin to change for the better when people focus on what they already have as gifts and talents.* Treasure wasn't sure what the answer was, but knowing Professor Pittman, he knew it had something to do with purpose and destiny because that was all she talked about, if she wasn't teaching biology. He thought of Simone and how she fitted into the riddle.

Time evaporated like vapour in the wind when he read the story. Just like the song, the story sparked light into his dark world and gave him a sense of purpose. Like a subsiding tempest, the story and the song brought tranquillity to the furious hurricane within him, giving him something to strive and to fight for, with all his might. It gave him a Journey to undertake and it sparked a switch of enlightenment inside of him. He knew he had to do something, he was reckless and he could feel something burning within his spirit. He felt motivated, inspired. What Treasure didn't know is that he was having an epiphany.

Full of mirth in his heart, Treasure strolled outside to help his mother plough and sow vegetable seeds in their home food garden, even though the earth was hard and dusty. The heat licked his mother's sunburnt face and looped around her limbs like a huge warm-blooded snake. The ground smouldered and emitted a perplexing steam. Even the birds were not chirping as much as they should have and the grass stood brown and hard.

Treasure thought his mother was the most beautiful mother in the world. Mrs Wedu, his guardian, saw him as the apple of her eye and he saw her with the same kind of light. The people knew her for the love she had for her children, she loved her husband even though he was a drunk and she loved her humble abode. Indeed, she did build the house herself, with mudbricks and timber. Mrs Wedu was scrawny and gaunt, although her appearance was fetching and the adorable dimples on her cheeks were as cuddly as a panda bear cub. She always smiled and her humility was forever present, her gentleness and kindness were like piercings on her ears – it stuck with her wherever she went.

The daily picking and digging of the soil in her backyard, like a treasure hunter digging for treasure and the monotonous torture of the sun, burnt her fair skin bronze. There was no sign of rain, but she ploughed and sowed anyway.

Outside her house, on the footpath that crossed below Mrs Wedu's house, were two women returning from the drying well, with clay jugs of water on their heads. Both of them were wearing traditional habesha kemis dresses with hand woven head wraps, matching the colour of the design on the front. One dress had orange flowery designs on the chest and the other had a green design. "There she is again," murmured one of the woman under her breath, nudging the other. "The famine has made her really mad. Can't she see she's wasting her time. There's not even a cloud in the sky, but she still digs like a mad man," she chuckled. "It's the second year now… and still there's no sign of anything happening," they gossiped, giggling softly and nudging each other.

The other woman shushed the other and shouted Mrs Wedu's name, "Liya," she yelled. Mrs Wedu turned around and greeted them, waving with a placid smile, balancing her weight on the pick, with one hand resting on her hip.

"How's it going with the harvest?" the woman in orange shouted. "Is there anything showing yet?"

Mrs Wedu shook her head, "No, but soon something is going to happen. Is there any water left in the well?"

The women in orange shook her head, "Not much," she said. "We can almost see the ground now."

"It will rain soon," said Mrs Wedu. "And the wells will fill up to overflow again."

The two women looked at each other amused and snorted out giggles. They didn't believe that and they thought her faith was a joke. They chortled, "Well, one day we will join you," the woman in orange said.

"Yes," the woman in green assented. "I'm sure it's going to be a great produce," she continued, scoffing and dripping with sarcasm. "When the harvest is plenty, you should share with us too."

Mrs Wedu chuckled and said she would indeed share with them, "Trust me, a miracle is going to happen this year."

The woman at the back nudged the one in the front so she could walk; they thought Mrs Wedu was starting with foolish talk. "Well, good luck with that," shouted the woman in orange, "and all the best."

"Well, that's *if* something happens," the other woman whispered, turning her head away and they both giggled simultaneously covering their mouths.

"Thank you," Mrs Wedu shouted and stared at them as they sashayed away shaking their hips, laughing like little girls. They're making a fool out of me, Mrs Wedu thought. They really think I'm an idiot. Perhaps the famine and drought doesn't affect them as bad as it does me and my kids. Mrs Wedu shook her head, "I don't care what they say or think," she murmured to herself. "One day the rain will come… All women are created equal, but some women work harder in preseason."

Treasure was standing at the little wooden gate at the garden that hung on its hinges, listening and he felt his heart growing heavier. He wished his mother could take a break because she worked too hard on the garden every day and there was not much rain. When Mrs Wedu saw Treasure walking towards her and picking up the shovel to help her, she smiled jutting her perfect piano teeth. Treasure chuckled and threw his gaze up to heave, noticing a little cloud, no bigger than a man's hand.

She knew he was mocking her, so she chuckled and said, "So you also think I'm crazy now, eh?" she said and shook her head, then continued digging with the pick. "Don't worry my boy, the rain will come. Maybe not today, but it will come… All we need to do is to keep on digging and sowing our seeds, even though we look like fools." She erected her body again and placed her hands on her hips. "One day, I will tell you the story of a man called Noah who built an ark preparing for a big flood to come and gathered all the animals and his family… to the other people of the community, Noah looked like a fool, until the day it began to rain and the flood started. Everybody wanted to get into the ark, but it was too late… So we will look like fools, until the rain comes."

Treasure smiled, shook his head and thrust the shovel into the soil, dredging it down with his foot, "You know what I believe Imayē?" he asked. (Imayē means *Mum* in Amharic)

Mrs Wedu ceased what she was doing, standing upright and listened.

Treasure looked up into the sky, "the Americans will come and save us," he said in a dreamy state. "Like Professor Pittman, they will all come like her and save us. The will help us rebuild our village and the whole of Ethiopia will be saved. They will come and drop food with big aeroplanes. They will bring some more doctors like Professor Pittman to help us." This was Treasure's dream.

Mrs Wedu smiled and said, "Indeed wenidi liji," she said. "Is that your dream wenidi liji?" she continued asking. (wenidi liji means *son* in Amharic)

Treasure nodded, "Yes, Imayē," he said. He thought about the story of the Young King and Queen then broodingly said, "I want to change Sululta, build wells for water, plant food gardens in every house in Ethiopia, heal sick children and become a doctor in America," his smile extended to his ear as he poured out his dreams to the person he trusted with his life. "You know what else Imayē?"

"What else wenidi liji?"

"I want to find my purpose," Treasure said, "and change the world like Professor Pittman. I want to leave my mark, so *everyone* would know, I was here," he stared at her for a moment and said, "I don't belong here Imayē," he said and looked up to the heavens, "there's more for me out there. I want to do something, I want to be somebody and I want to go somewhere Imayē. I want to be like Ms Rosa Parks, Nelson Mandela and Martin Luther and die empty…" Treasure was almost in a weeping state when he uttered these words.

His mother looked at him with eyes filled with awe, admiration and pride. She felt the words permeate from deep within his heart. She trembled as the goose pimples radiated through her body. She smiled at him with a broad smile, "you've got very big dreams, yenē wenidi liji," she said. "And big dreams do come true." (Yenē wenidi liji means *My Son* in Amharic)

Treasure's face dropped, "But I'm afraid Imayē?"

"Afraid of what?"

He gulped staring at her, "…What if I never find my purpose? What if I take the wrong path or do the wrong thing?"

His mother smiled tilting her head sideways beaming with a bit of empathy, considering that he's still just a little boy, "Wenidi liji," she said in a soft tone. "If it's not the right path or the right thing, then it will be the path that will lead you to the thing you want… We are all blindfolded. But the most important thing is to take the first step, even in the dark and just do it."

There was a slight pause between them, "Why don't you ask me what my dream is…?" Mrs Wedu probed.

Treasure chuckled, "I'd love to know your dream Ma."

She smiled scanning her eyes through the garden, "I don't want much… But if there's something I want for the world, is love, peace and compassion," she said.

Treasure nodded.

"But I have another one," she said. "When I die… bury me here, in this garden."

Treasure frowned. He hated it when she spoke about death. He couldn't imagine her dying, "You're not gonna die Ma, so don't talk like that. I will study, get a job, go to America and become a Doctor… and buy you a house."

Mrs Wedu smiled, "Thank you son," she said. "I like that. But you know, the risk of death hangs over our heads as well. One day we will die. Death is a part of life and so is suffering. No one gets a free pass from those two things, no one…" she said. "You're a very nice boy, but not even you... One day, you will suffer without me. And thinking about us approaching death can be life-changing. People who think that they will one day die, actually behave in healthier ways – and therefore may actually live longer," she added and chuckled. "So don't worry, I won't die, until you're strong enough to live without me… To think this way may seem bad, but it provides us with a proper and realistic view of life. To live fully, we must be aware of our limitations and most worthy of attention is the scarcity and uncertain duration of time we have each been granted… you said Professor Pittman always says…?"

Treasure chuckled, "You only live once, but if you do it right, once is enough."

Mrs Wedu nodded, "She's right son," she said smiling broadly. "So remember, time does not belong to you. You only have one life, only one. So make it meaningful and one way to do that, is to be like me… use your gift and passion every day, because that is what you've been called for. Far too many people waste a great deal of time on doing things that contribute little of positive value to their lives and the lives of others… But you don't have to be one of those people. Help someone, do something special for people and leave your mark in this world, no matter how little it is," she said and chuckled. "Even if it's gardening."

They stared at each other smiling and continued digging. Mrs Wedu had a treasured talent for agriculture. She had faith in the seeds that she spent her life sowing and the confidence of a caterpillar. She expected to, one-day, morph and flutter into the bright light of the sun, forgetting about all the dry and barren days of her life. The stench of sweat always lingered on her like the citrus scent of a lemon, as though she dug the Lega Dembi mines, like her husband used to. Nevertheless, she couldn't care less; she was digging, picking and scrapping for food for her children, much like a cheetah mother does when she raises her young.

Amongst the Sululta people, it was common for a woman to smell like a man, work like a man, provide like a man and love, support and cherish like a wife and a mother. Her dirtied skin was a sure sign of rough living, not to mention the worn-out clothes she wore – most likely handed down from one of the neighbours.

Her old house must have been little more than a glorified shed, even in its heyday. It looked as if a giant had sat on the roof, for it sagged dreadfully. The windows had gaping holes in which the wind rushed in and out and the door hung at a jaunty angle. It was a rotting heap, surrendering to the elements. Nevertheless, she saw treasure in her trash and tried her utmost to make her humble abode a safe house, a beautiful place and a home for her children. It was beautiful to her because she built it.

***

AFTER THE DAY'S HARD WORK, ploughing, digging and scrapping the soil, Mrs Wedu and Treasure sat in the dining room, whilst Treasure read out aloud to Mrs Wedu from the book *When Rain Clouds Gather* by Bessie Head. She loved the story; she had an utter fondness for the title. She couldn't read well, but she understood English very well after spending time with Professor Pittman, helping her in her garden, when she first came to Sululta.

She gazed and marvelled in Treasure's eyes, looking at him and beaming with admiration as he read the story to her, admiring him as if he were Johann Chrysostom Wolfgang Amadeus Mozart, some kind of prodigy. She thought that Treasure came to epitomise classical storytelling in its purity of form and style. She stroked his hair, smiling endearingly and said, "One day you're going to be the president of this country."

Treasure chuckled and dropped his gaze, "C'mon Ma," he said and shrugged, "it's just a story. Anybody can do this."

Mrs Wedu shook her head, "No, my boy. Not anybody. This is a gift. If you're saying anybody, it means you're including me too…?

Treasure glanced at her as though he had said something wrong and back to the book because he knew she couldn't read English, but only speak it.

"…and I can't do this," she said. "Many people may be able to do it. But they might not do it like you… Listen my boy, what makes a person gifted and talented may not always be good grades in school, but a different way of looking at life, learning and doing things in their own unique way…" she lifted up his hand, "like the finger prints on your fingers, they will never match anybody else's. You have a unique talent and I can see your efforts and effort beats talent every time and you have both." She beckoned her head to the book, "This is your gift." She stroked him behind his head. "I feel blessed for having you. You have so much wisdom, you're smart, strong – no one can ever be you."

Treasure gazed deeply into her eyes, gulped, nodded a little and continued reading, "… and I don't care about people. I don't care about anything, not even the white man. I want to…"

BANG! The door opened, slamming against the wall. Treasure and Mrs Wedu flinched. It was Treasure's father stumbling at the door with a beer bottle, his gaze dropped, rocking back and forth.

"It's fine son," Mrs Wedu said, trying to remain composed. "Continue reading."

Treasure continued and mumbled some words. The door shutting again interrupted him, "I'm hungry," Mr Wedu barked.

As Treasure tried to read on, he sensed a piercing stare from the man he called his father. He felt Mr Wedu's thoughts knot together as the urge to hurt him, poisoned his blood. A hunger, crumbled his insides as he staggered forward, with vicious eyes and a condescending smirk.

Angry eyes were just the start, then came the cursing, the slamming and the demanding of food and money. His rage built up like deep-water currents. He was always in a bad mood.

"Didn't you hear what I said boy," Mr Wedu hissed, leaning forward. "Go, get me some food."

"There is no food," Treasure said tight-faced, with a dropped gaze.

"Leave him alone," Mrs Wedu said. "I don't remember the last time you brought food into this house… continue reading son."

Mr Wedu's jaw went into a spasm, "Are you disrespecting me, woman?" he growled.

Before Mrs Wedu could even get the words out of her mouth, Mr Wedu blew a backhand through her face that sent her right of the couch.

Treasure jumped up and wrestled Mr Wedu, shouting for him to leave his mother alone. Mr Wedu overpowered Treasure and punched him in the mouth, sending him against the wall. Mr Wedu pounced towards Treasure and straddled him, growling and groaning like a mad man. Mrs Wedu whimpered on the floor struggling to hoist herself up, writhing and wincing out of pain.

There was blood on Mr Wedu's knuckles, Treasure's nose was gushing with blood and his eyes became bruised, almost immediately. They were watery, red stained and he heard a cracking noise on his jaw. Mr Wedu didn't stop until he saw blood. When both of them were bleeding and lying worthlessly on the ground, he sniggered, "I will kill you, both of you!" he said and kicked Treasure's foot, "stupid boy," then staggered out of the door to his bedroom whilst murmuring, growling, grunting, groaning and scowling then he trailed off as he bounced back and forth on the walls.

All that Treasure desired was to protect his mother from his father and to erase his family's name from the books of poverty and misery.

The young man dreamt about a better life. He hoped for a bright future. He saw himself and his family out of poverty, he saw himself leading people and changing lives. He dreamt of noble things, he thought of intelligence, of refinement, of grace and beauty. He dreamt about holding gigantic responsibilities with unequal influence. He dreamt of speaking and witnessing lives change in front of his eyes. His soul burnt to achieve this professed ideal.

Treasure and his mother leaned on each other against the wall. Mother and son, both bleeding. Her husband was no longer the man she married. After he lost his job, he became a drunkard, plain and simple. His breakfast was cheap vodka and beer. Sometimes he drank anything to keep himself from being sober. Every day by lunchtime, he passed out and by the afternoon, he would be longing for more spirits. His temper was legendary. He detested himself and anyone who showed him kindness.

5

Every minute, THREE children died.

The next day Treasure remained in bed, unable to get up. His face ached like broken bones. His nose was hammered and cracked, both eyes were swollen and blue and a red dot of blood had formed on the sclera, with his iris and pupil swollen as well.

When he stared into a sharp light, it felt like a needle piercing through his eye. Every few minutes he grunted. The pain had a raw kind of quality, brutal. Being beaten by an old man, as if you were an old man yourself is not an easy thing to go through if you're just a teenager. Something ached inside him. Something felt so out of place. *When will this suffering stop?* he thought. It was something dredged deep, deep in the abyss of his soul.

He stared at himself in his wardrobe mirror, buttoning his shirt. His reflection in the mirror reflected a boy he had never imagined, never even seen in a nightmare. It felt so painful that his vision, did not match his reality. 'Has someone cursed or bewitched my family and me?' he thought. 'Am I the cause of my parents fighting every day? Am I to blame for what is happening to my family? Does my father hate me because I'm different and not like the other boys? Is there something that life is punishing me for?' Maybe karma had come home to roost.

He glanced up at a black and white picture of Friedrich Nietzsche, which he had pinned above his wardrobe mirror. Next to the picture was a quote reading, *'To Live is to suffer, to survive is to find some meaning in the suffering.'* He said the words as he read them. The quote always reminded him, *to persevere through pain.*

After getting dressed for school, Treasure walked inside the kitchen with all the muscles on his face tensed up. His mother had just finished preparing breakfast for him. Well it was barely breakfast. It was two sloppy spoons of oatmeal. He ate it every single day of his life, like a cow eating grass, so he hated the sight and the smell of it. Just the sight of it made him queasy. He hungered for something else to eat for once, something different, something more nourishing that would make him wiggle his toes and dance.

His mother gazed at his face and she felt a heavy knob in her throat and tears gathered in her eyes, "I made you some porridge," she said in a doleful tone.

Treasure glanced at the bowl, screwed his face as though he was looking at something disgusting and shook his head, whilst scooping some water in a cup, "No thank you," he said gimlet-eyed, dropping his head after drinking from the cup. There was some distance between Mrs Wedu and Treasure. He kept looking away, but she kept trying to turn his face to see the bruises on his face, "I'm fine," he said exasperated and pulled his face away.

"I just want to see," Mrs Wedu said trying to turn his face towards her again.

"I'm fine, Imayē," he said again and walked to the table, packed some schoolbooks he had left on the table the night before and ferociously shoved them inside his tattered school bag, patched with different colours and types of fabrics, to close the holes. His face was tight and his eyebrows were bumped in a scowl.

She stared at him for a while, with her head tilted to one side and her lips set in a grim line, "At least eat something son," she said. "You'll collapse in front of those kids."

Without much mortification, Treasure threw his school bag over his shoulder, yanked the kitchen doorknob and dust sprinkled from the doorframe, "I'm not hungry," he snapped. "I'll see you later."

Just when he was about to slam the door shut, his mother called him back.

Vexed to the brim, Treasure gasped, throwing his gaze upwards, clinching his jaw, "What Imayē? I said I'm not hungry," he groaned.

Even though she knew Treasure was erratic and oblivious, this morning she could sense that different emotions were raging through him. She wanted to tell him the truth about her and his father. Maybe he would better understand why his 'father' treated him that way; it was not his son and she was not his mother, but the words couldn't leave her mouth, she was afraid of losing him. As great as courage could be, it also had its risks. She gulped, with a troubled heart pounding through her chest and her countenance dropped, "Rest," she croaked, her voice doleful, "you don't have to go to school today. I'll go to your principal and tell him you're sick-"

"NO," he retorted. "*I'm going.* We're writing tests next week… I'll see you later." He banged the door before she could convince him otherwise and walked away with long strides and heavy treads.

She knew the kids would add to his pain by laughing at him. Mrs Wedu sighed and deflated, "God, why?" she prayed, "How do I tell him? How do I help him?"

***

THE WIND HOWLED AS THE students arrived through the school gates, hustling and bustling down the dusty grounds of the schoolyard. Friends greeted each other with hugs and playful punches while Treasure sat at the bench alone downcast, looking scared and depressed. The seniors stood, tall and proud.

When his peers saw his face they started nudging each other and pointing at him. Treasure tried to hold a straight face. One of the biggest school bullies, Kidane, one of the seniors, laughed cockily at him, "Mr Wedu," Kidane said with a contemptuous smile and tone. Treasure glanced at him with a dark look, eyes bumped together in a scowl.

Kidane sniggered looking at his friends and turned towards Treasure lifting three fingers, "How many fingers am I holding?" His friends giggled and laughed with their arms crossed, looking down their noses at Treasure.

Treasure stared at them with a fixed countenance and walked towards his classroom.

"Did you forget to duck?" Kidane said, pleased and happy to see Treasure looked that way. They mocked him saying his father used him as his punching bag and Kidane threw a scrambled piece of paper against Treasure's head.

Treasure froze, looking down with his jaw clenched. His hands folded into a tight fist, he felt his heart beating faster and he wanted to punch Kidane in the face. He exhaled, closing his eyes, "It's not worth it," a voice inside of him said and he walked away.

"How could you lose to someone who trips over his own feet? Even a toddler can beat your father up," Kidane said, ridiculing him but Treasure continued walking.

When Treasure entered the classroom, his classmates, murmured, scoffed and jeered behind his back as if he was not there. They murmured and giggled amongst themselves and laughed hysterically at him.

Every time they opened their mouths, his anger went up like a coolant temperature gauge on an old car. His fist clenched so hard his knuckles turned pale. He felt his face heating up, his jaw clenched tight because the words they called him were sour. Beneath his desk, he pumped his legs up and down on his toes rapidly.

Professor Pittman sighed and her body slumped when she saw him walk into the classroom. Treasure couldn't look her in her eyes. Her sadness was like a running stream, cold and endless. It cleansed all the virtue out of her and left her a trifling shell.

She cleared her throat, "Take your seats, take your seats," she ordered to her scholars. 'I'll be checking your homework in a minute, but before I start, I wanted to share something with you guys." The kids began to settle down in their seats and the conversations began to cease. Finally when silence reigned, she said, "I'm not going to take much of your time, but I want you to use your imaginations a bit… I want you to close your eyes…"

The scholars began closing their eyes, some were still a bit confused about what she was asking.

"All of you," she added, "Just close your eyes for a moment…" she waited until all the scholars' eyes were shut. "Now picture an empty vase or pot with a crack down the middle… Can you see it?"

The scholars nodded, but some didn't.

"Now," she continued. "Just imagine that the pot is filled with a very bright light… and I cover the vase with my hand or the lid… Where do you think the light will shine through?"

The kids were silent, afraid to answer and not sure of the correct answer. The class was eerily quiet.

"C'mon now, I know you know the answer," Professor Pittman said, scanning her eyes across the class looking for a raised hand. "Anybody can answer, c'mon now…"

The kids were still silent.

"Okay, I'm gonna choose someone, err… Simone!" she said, touching her shoulders.

Simone's heart galloped, she didn't like being in the spot light. She gulped, trembled, "T-The crack?" she croaked softly, stammering.

"YES," Professor Pittman blurted out, pumping her fist. "Simone is right… it's the crack. Okay, you can open your eyes now."

The scholars' eyes began popping open as they blinked.

"Everything broken in your life," Professor Pittman said, "every crack in your life, every pain, every adversity, every struggle, every disappointment, is all just a crack in a vase… However, if you have a little light inside your vase, if you have a purpose, burning inside of you, the light of your purpose will shine through the broken parts in your life."

She scanned their faces and specifically Treasure, who was listening attentively but had his face glued down to his desk.

"Don't fold to the darkness of life," Professor Pittman said. "Don't break, don't bow, don't be afraid, don't let it intimidate you, don't let it kill the light in you. Only one thing can cut out darkness… and that's light. The light in you can light up your world and light up the world for other people as well. The provisions of struggles, pain, trials and tribulations are always blessings in disguise. When you are trying to change your life, you will face some sort of challenge in one way or another, but it is part of the process… People can turn off all the lights and still there will always be a blazing flame in your soul, always burning for love, always ready to start a new blaze, always ready to live and chase after destiny."

The scholars were silent as usual, listening attentively.

"Now," Professor Pittman said and clapped her hands, "the fun is over, take out your homework and Biology books."

The class murmured, wishing she could talk on for longer.

Professor Pittman droned on about atoms, nucleus this and electron that. Although Treasure was distracted, his attention never drifted far off to the extent of making him absent. Professor Pittman noticed a spark of an idea or inspiration flicker in Treasure's eyes – and to kindle it she cold-called him and asked him a question. "Treasure," she said, "tell us everything you know about a nucleus."

Treasure cleared the slime from his throat, "Ehem, err, uhm…"

Kidane laughed, "He doesn't know Professor. His father knocked the sense out of him."

The class chorused in laughter.

Professor Pittman didn't smirk or smile and ignored the brutish comment, "C'mon anything…?" she said moving forward towards Treasure's desk.

Treasure gulped, "Well, the nucleus is the largest cellular organelle in animal cells," he explained. "In mammalian cells, the average diameter of the nucleus is approximately six micrometres, which occupies about ten percent of the total cell volume. The viscous liquid within it is called nucleoplasm and is similar in composition to the cytosol found outside the nucleus. It appears as a dense, roughly spherical or irregular organelle. The composition-"

Professor Pittman raised her hand, smiling proudly of him, "That's enough my boy," she said, smiling and nudged Kidane. "I guess Treasure has just knocked some sense into you, huh?"

The class muttered whispers and giggles while Kidane grimaced with embarrassment, scratching his head like a chimpanzee with fleas.

"Well done, Treasure," Professor Pittman said backing up towards the black chalkboard. "You are right indeed. The nucleus is indeed the largest cellular organelle in animal mammals…" Professor Pittman trailed off and elaborated on what Treasure had said.

Simone gazed at Treasure, beaming, smiling and inspired. She unconsciously gazed at him like he was some kind of all-conquering hero. She tucked her braids behind her ears and looked away abruptly when her eyes met with Treasure's. She felt a lightning bolt jolting through her body.

Treasure's stomach growled loudly and he squirmed on his seat trying to cover the sound of the rumbling with his arms by tucking his stomach in and softy screeching his chair on the floor. He glanced at the clock on the wall; two more minutes left until school was out.

Professor Pittman droned on, but Treasure's head was now preoccupied with what was happening inside his gut. He fantasised gulping down mouthfuls of water at the school tap. He was already salivating at the thought of it. *Only one minute left.* He tapped his legs up and down with his toes and watched the clock as the red seconds' hand slowly completed its circle around the clock. The closer it got, the slower it seemed to go. His stomach rumbled again, louder and he tried to cover it with his hand, bending down and uttering a little prayer in his mind. No one heard the loud noise, except Simone. She pretended as if she did not hear anything. The bell rang. He had never been happier in his life.

He stormed out of the classroom, as if something was on fire and ran to the school's well, threw his tie over his shoulders and opened the tap like a fire-fighter. When the first gush of water splashed in his stomach, he could feel it first sink in and then swell up in his stomach like a balloon filling up with water. He could feel himself regaining his strength. He drank like a Scottish man drinking beer, as though he was drinking for the next generation. Behind him, grew a long line of students waiting to drink. They fretted and complained, but Treasure was not bothered, he continued drinking like a camel. If it were not for his tie, which flipped over in front of the water, he would not have stopped.

He stood up and placed his hands on his hips panting, huffing and puffing as if he had just done the one hundred-metre sprint. His head tilted up, his mouth open, dripping with water down his chin, "Sorry guys," he gasped.

They looked at him with their cheeks puffed out in anger. One girl with her arms folded clicked her tongue, "He's doing it on purpose."

"He's undermining us," another girl added.

"He thinks he's so clever," one boy added, "and better than everyone."

People always told him that he thought he was better. Those words were his 'Hello,' he heard them so often they had stopped bothering him. In fact, many things had stopped bothering him, like the fact that he almost had no friends. He knew many people and many people knew him, but the more they knew him, the more they disliked him.

***

LATER THAT AFTERNOON WHEN TREASURE arrived at Professor Pittman's house, she was outside in her garden busy preparing the soil for her new food garden project which Mrs Wedu was helping her with.

Professor Pittman saw Treasure entering the gate, "Ah, you're here," she blurted out in a very enthusiastic and eager manner. "Your mother was just here helping me prepare the soil…gosh she has some real talent."

Treasure chuckled, "Yeah, she surely does. All she does all day is work in the garden."

Professor Pittman nodded, "Well, she has a gift," she said, taking off her green, dirty gardening gloves and beckoned with her hand, "C'mon inside, I'll make you some coffee."

They walked inside the house and Treasure followed her, whilst glancing at the spitted garden soil. He gulped fearfully, thinking that his mother had taken it too far now. He thought she was good doing the gardening at their house, but not helping other people because there was no rain. She was making a fool of herself and people were laughing at her and even his peers were mocking him because of it.

They entered Professor Pittman's house. Her house was made of mud, sticks, plastered with cement and coated with creamy paint. The house had two bedrooms, a kitchen and a dining area with many books. She used one bedroom for sleeping and the other bedroom as a medical ward. So the house always smelt like a hospital and there was always that rumbling sound of the generator in the backyard and soft music playing.

Upon entering the house, Professor Pittman grunted and exhaled in exhaustion, placing her gloves on the kitchen table, "I'm glad you came, Treasure," she said, washing her hands in the clay basin. She had a two litre PET plastic bottle tied to the roof filled with water that she would tip over so the water would flow down in little streams as if it was a tap into a basin. She would then take the water, boil it and reuse it. Treasure always thought that this was extremely smart; in fact, he had started to build his own at home. "I have a lot to teach you today."

Treasure smiled, "I'm ready Professor… How's Lelo today?"

Professor Pittman exhaled through compressed lips, "She's sleeping, but she's getting better," she said, unpromising. "But I still haven't got her to eat yet. And worst of all, we're running out of multivitamin supplies." She pulled the little bar fridge freezer door and pulled out a little frozen bag of green peas and extended it to Treasure, "Here, put that on your eye… Have some tea and cookies and I'll make you sandwiches."

Treasure took the ice and pressed it on his black eye and again on his lip. "Thank you, I'll have it when we're done with Lelo."

Lelo was a little baby girl who Professor Pittman had taken into her house to take care of. She usually did this with little orphaned babies who lost their mothers, due to the sickness plague. Little Lelo had her ribs poking out of her stomach. She was undersized and Treasure thought she was as big as the video camera Professor Pittman gave him for his birthday; in fact, the video camera weighed more than Lelo. Little Lelo had an old-looking face with sunken eyes and cheeks, with loose skin. She had little fragile, bony legs and arms, with a bloated stomach. Her hair was brownish, chunks of it were falling out and she cried severely.

"Well, let's get started," Professor Pittman said and walked out of the kitchen into the passage that led to Lelo's room. "You know, you need to begin to take care of yourself, instead of taking care of everybody else except yourself, young man," she said with her head turned to the side. She always wore her blue medical scrub and always had her stethoscope dangling out of the side pocket.

Treasure ignored her and continued scanning his eyes through Professor Pittman's adventure pictures pinned on the wall.

Professor Pittman trailed off, "You can't always be there for everybody except yourself. Sometimes you have to help yourself first, before you can help other people," she said before opening the door that led to Lelo's room, staring at him for him to respond.

Treasure nodded and placed the frozen peas pack on the wooden table next to the door. He wanted her to treat him like a grown man, so he thought she was saying this because she thought he was a child. She sacrificed her life for everyone else, except herself, so if she could do it, so could he.

The smell of anti-bacterial detergents and medicine lingered in the house, even on her clothes. "Go wash your hands," Professor Pittman said, pulling out a pair of latex gloves from the box on the table. "And do it properly and put on your scrub," she brandished the gloves in the air, "and your gloves," she said and walked inside Lelo's room, closing the door behind her. She had a set of rules that she had pinned down on the table for Treasure to read before he could work with Lelo but she repeated them to him every day and sometimes, Treasure would mimic the rules back to her in his head.

Dear Treasure

Things to do before Care giving

Proper hand washing is very simple, requiring only the following basic steps:

1. Wet your hands with running water.
2. Apply liquid soap (if available) and scrub vigorously, for at least 10-15 seconds. (In situations where caretakers don't have access to clean, running water, a water-less antiseptic agent should be used.)
2. Pay special attention to nails, between fingers and around rings.
3. Rinse thoroughly under warm, running water.
4. Dry with a paper towel or clean cloth. Avoid using a towel, which can put germs back onto your clean hands.
5. Close the tap with the paper towel, not your hand.

Treasure rolled up his sleeves, tipped the little container mounted on the wall that made the water flow in a small stream, then washed, squirted some pink liquid soap onto his hands and began scouring with the brush in the clay basin.

After washing his hands, he unhooked a blue scrub from a hook hanger mounted on the wall and slipped his arms in one after the other while writhing, grunting and wincing in pain. He had bruises at the side of his rib cage.

He pulled a pair of white latex gloves out of the box, slipped them onto his hands, placed a surgical mask over his mouth and nose and then walked inside the room. This always made him feel like he was also a doctor.

Sometimes Lelo smelt so bad, Treasure had to run out and vomit in the basin, especially when she had puked and pooped on herself.

Treasure gulped as he stood next to Professor Pittman and she began instructing him on the procedures. No matter how good Treasure became, she still explained it to him as if it was his first day caregiving a little baby. She instructed him on how to bed bath wash her properly, how to feed her and give her medication and vitamins. Then he did some housework together with Professor Pittman. Caregiving little Lelo made him laser focused. Time would vanish when he was helping her, cleaning her, feeding her from the nanny bottle and spooning porridge into her mouth.

BED Bath rules

A bed bath is done to help wash someone who cannot get out of bed.

What supplies are needed for a bed bath?
Keep the following within easy reach:

Separate water basins and washcloths to wash and rinse
Bath towels
Soap, lotion, and deodorant
Lightweight blanket
Clean clothes

BED Bath rules

How do I give a bed bath?
Always make sure the person cannot fall out of bed if you need to walk away.
Wet the washcloth without soap. Gently wipe one eyelid by wiping from the inner corner of the eye to the outer corner. Pat the eyelid dry and repeat on the other eyelid.
With soap and water, wash and dry the person's face, neck, and ears.
Wash 1 side of the body from head to toe and then repeat on the other side. Pull the blanket or towel back while you wash, and cover when you are done. Start by washing the shoulder, upper body, arm, and hand. Move to the hip, legs, and feet. Rinse each area free from soap and pat dry before moving to the next. Check for redness and sores during the bed bath

BED Bath rules

Change the bath water before you wash the genital area.
The genital area is the last area to be washed. You may need to bend the person's knees to help reach the area better.
For little girls, wash the genital area from front to back. (but I will wash the little girls)For little boys, make sure you wash around the testicles. To clean between the buttocks, you may need to help the person roll onto his side.

Professor Pittman also gave Treasure a book on Child Nutrition and a Paediatric First Aid for Caregivers toolkit, she had compiled from sources from the International Federation of Red Cross and Red Crescent Societies, cutting out pictures, then making a collage from them.

"First aid skills are for everyone," she said. "You're a caregiver now, a world changer. If you study and pay very close attention to everything I'm teaching you, you'll be a hero and save many lives."

Treasure nodded, "Yes, Ma'am." He heeded the advice and continued to listen attentively.

"One day, you'll be able to teach these things to everyone in Sululta," Professor Pittman said, smiling whilst she rubbed some more lotion on little Lelo's tiny arms, "and save millions of babies."

Treasure felt his heart dance. None of his peers knew the things that Professor Pittman was teaching him privately.

"What we're doing now is capacity building," Professor Pittman said.

Out of confusion, Treasure frowned and squinted his eyes, "And what's that?" he croaked.

Professor Pittman chuckled, "I'm sorry, Treasure," she said feeling stupid, "sometimes I forget you're just a kid… Well, right now I'm helping you develop the ability to act independently, so that you will be capable of helping solve the problem of dying babies in the community. Well, capacity building is building new skills to make you capable of doing new things."

Treasure nodded.

"But it doesn't end there," Professor Pittman added. "After that you will have to teach other people how to do the same things you're doing. You will need to develop a team. Do you remember what the Young King and Queen did in the story I gave you?"

Treasure nodded, "Yes, Professor."

"They began working together, using their different skills, we call them their capacity," she said and chuckled, "or you can call it their treasure," she said.

Treasure chuckled through his nose.

"Ironic isn't it?"

Treasure nodded.

She continued, "The Young King and Queen built capacity," she said, "which is the ability to be capable to do something and act. It helped them to find food, build shelter and get off the Island… just as we're doing now. And when they did that, they achieved what is called, Social Capital."

Treasure frowned again; the terms all sounded almost the same to him.

Professor Pittman chuckled, "Don't worry," she said. "Every time you have a problem understanding, refer back to the story alright? I didn't give you the story for nothing. But, you'll learn about it pretty soon," she finished dressing Lelo up in new clean and warmer clothes, positioning her little body on the bed. She stuck a milk bottle in Lelo's mouth and watched Lelo begin to suck at it, looking at her as if Lelo was the most precious thing she'd ever seen. "Isn't she beautiful," Professor Pittman said, amiably with tears glittering in her eyes.

Treasure smiled back.

Professor Pittman looked deep into Treasure's eyes, smiling at him, whilst little Lelo fiddled with her tiny legs making sucking noises sucking on her bottle. "Right now, this is a perfect example of social capital… me and you using our gifts and talents helping each other to save little Lelo. It's a relationship between people who live together, which helps them to work together in such a way as to achieve a desired result."

Treasure saw a light bulb beam at the top of his head. He remembered how the Young King and Queen worked together to find food, build a house, make a fire and meet their needs.

Professor Pittman could see it in his face that he began to understand, as his eyes lit up and his facial muscles became more relaxed. She continued, "The result of us working together as a team, will lead to little Lelo getting better every day and that will helps us move on to help other little dying babies… and this is called the community development outcome," she said and paused, staring at him to see if he was still confused. "Do you wish to guess what community development outcome is…?"

Treasure brooded, gathering his thoughts, putting his thinking hat on.

"Remember what I said," Professor Pittman said. "Go back to the story of the Young King and Queen. What is the last thing that they achieved…?"

Treasure brooded and another light bulb beamed at the top of his head. Using his imagination, just like Professor Pittman had taught them, he closed his eyes and went back to the story of the Young King and Queen. BOOM, he remembered, "I know Professor," he said, smiling. "When the Young King and Queen worked together using their skills and talents, they were able to find food, build a house, have a good meal and sleep," he said and paused to see whether he was on the right track by judging Professor Pittman's expression.

Professor Pittman nodded, "Yeah, continue."

"It's rising up and building the fabric of your own society," Treasure added. "Working together and taking action, which leads to things getting better and that's the community development outcome"

Professor Pittman smiled and patted Treasure's arm, "Excellent!" she shrieked, proud of him. "You see, you know this now."

Treasure grinned broadly showing all his teeth, his eyes crinkled. Every emotion was fleeting, every thought gave way to a new more positive thought. Learning was fun for him. He felt like there wasn't a reason to despair, but a good reason to rejoice. Now he could take all that Professor Pittman had taught him and help someone else.

What Treasure didn't know was that Professor Pittman was teaching him exactly what Mrs Wedu had taught her. How to live with a purpose. She knew that by instilling in him a sense of purpose, he would be able to triumph over all of his adversities, when he began striving to achieve big goals.

Professor Pittman trailed of teaching him about how to be able to screen a child for acute malnutrition by checking for oedema or using the mid-upper arm circumference (MUAC) tape; how to know if a child was acutely malnourished based on signs of oedema or MUAC interpretation and taught him to understand why and where a child with acute malnutrition should be referred.

Treasure knew this like the back of his hands, but still Professor Pittman monitored him closely when he measured the child's weight, length, height and mid-upper arm circumference with well-calibrated instruments.

Steps for screening using MUAC tape:

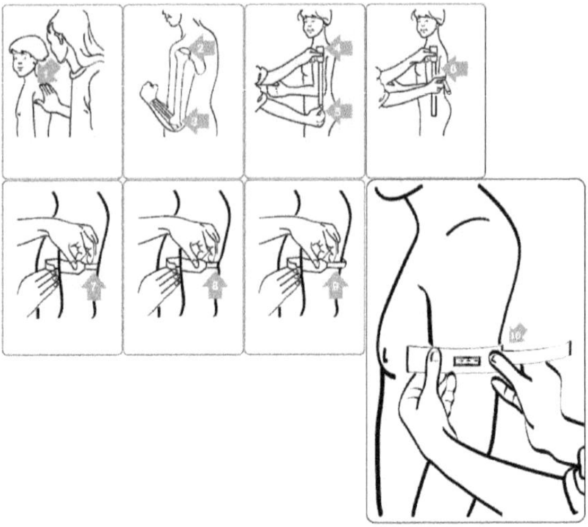

She taught him how to interpret MUAC indicators for children aged six months (over 65 cm) to five years (under 110 cm).

"I don't want you trying to do anything by yourself alright," Professor Pittman said. "We can't help the baby if it dies."

Treasure nodded.

"Refer children with severe acute malnutrition with oedema or any medical complications, listed in the infographic I gave you, to the clinics," she said. "But preferably to me or a designated nutrition rehabilitation unit for inpatient management."

Treasure wanted to do everything for the kids, he even wanted to make them feel better, "Why can't I help them first."

Professor Pittman shook her head, with a tight-lipped smile, "You shouldn't try Treasure. Children with severe acute malnutrition should undergo a full clinical evaluation to identify medical complications plus an 'appetite' test and that is more complicated than what we do here… but that's not to say your work isn't valuable."

She mussed his hair, "So tell me, what are the most important duties?"

Treasure looked up trying to gather his thoughts "Err," he began counting on his fingers. "Appropriate feeding practices and the advantages of continued breastfeeding. Feed the children safe, palatable foods with high-energy content and adequate micronutrients, which form the cornerstone of nutritional management."

"That's right," she said. "You're getting better every day."

Treasure LOVED doing this. His burning desire was to see little Lelo getting better and living a normal life again. He felt he had a purpose. Caregiving the sick children that Professor Pittman brought to her house was his anecdote to all the problems of his life. It was therapeutic to him, like a writer who finds healing in writing and a painter who finds the same in painting. It shut out the world for him and stilled the storm. It plunged him into his creative, genius zone and rejuvenated his ambitions.

***

AFTER TAKING CARE OF LELO and much learning, they sat at the dining room, sipping on tea and having cookies. Before Professor Pittman sank herself down on the sofa, she lit up the kerosene lamp, adjusting the wick with the burner sleeve.

"How does that work?" Treasure asked curiously.

"A flat-wick lamp has a fuel tank (fount), with the lamp burner attached… When the lamp is lit, the kerosene that the wick has absorbed burns and produces a clear, bright, yellow flame. As the kerosene burns, capillary action in the wick draws more kerosene up from the fuel tank… And that's how the light shines."

Treasure nodded but wondered how the fabric wick could draw the kerosene on it's own, "Will the wick be able to draw on water?" Treasure asked feeling an idea bubbling in his mind.

"Yeah," Professor Pittman said, "any fabric is able to absorb fluid."

Treasure saw a lightbulb beam at the top of his head. Professor Pittman had a stack of plastic bottles she collected from the United Nations Military officers. They always received canned food and beverages in plastic containers. She drove to UN Military camps, collected the empty containers, kept them in her house and reused them as baby feeding bottles. She had quite a number of them stacked in her dining room, her kitchen and her backyard.

This is the time when Professor Pittman would pour out her wisdom to Treasure, sometimes that's all he looked forward to. No matter how much he loved what he was doing, cleaning up Lelo's poop was the only thing he didn't look forward to.

Professor Pittman sank herself into the couch emitted a big sigh, "You know," Professor Pittman croaked, wearily, placing the cup on the saucer after taking a sip. "You will be rewarded for everything you're doing for little Lelo. Sometimes I look into Lelo's eyes and wish she could die to stop the pain, but then when I'm alone, all I want is for her to get better and live a normal life again, like every other kid."

Treasure clenched the cup with both hands, "She's getting better. I can watch her every day until she's healthy again," Treasure said, "so she doesn't get sick again."

Professor Pittman smiled amiably at Treasure with her head tilted to one side, astonished by his gift of generosity, "My boy, when it comes to someone's life, we can only do so much then the rest is left to the Creator. We just have to play our part, because we all have a part to play."

Treasure breathed out a deep breath. He didn't want Lelo to die like the other babies did, but Professor Pittman was trying to get him to understand that even if she died, he still added value to her life and played his part.

She took a sip of tea and sat up, "Your mother told me you've taught her how to read and write?"

Treasure chuckled and nodded humbly, "Yes Ma'am, I'm trying to. She reads my school books with me now."

"You see… I always told you, you're a genius!" Professor Pittman said and there was a pause in the conversation.

Professor Pittman sat upright, "You see, all these things happening in our community - famine, sickness, violence and poverty will never stop until everybody in the community, *rises up and builds the fabric of their own community*… I am tired of waiting for things to change. I'm tired of young people squandering every opportunity they have, wasting their lives on drugs, alcohol and sex. It's time for the young people to stand together and fight for their own future."

Treasure gulped, feeling the adrenaline surging through his body like an electric current. He couldn't figure out why she was saying all these things but he knew that there was a good purpose behind them.

She leaned forward, pulled the drawer at the side desk at the couch and pulled out a document typed with a typewriter. She held it in her hands as if it was a long lost manuscript of the greatest novel ever written. She hugged it, "I worked on this for many years," she said, "trying to come up with a plan that would help all the children of Ethiopia." She looked at the document.

"Everything in here contains the things that I wanted to do when I came back to Ethiopia." She gazed in his eyes for a moment, looking at him as though she was reading deep into his soul, she leaned forward and proffered the file to him and said, "Everything in here, I want you to do."

Treasure gulped, squinting his eyes at the front page of the document. Another word he didn't know leapt out to him on the front page - PROPOSAL. What in the living God was a proposal? The document was not thick or heavy, but she kept it safe even though the pages had turned a little yellow and dusty.

Professor Pittman chuckled, "Don't worry too much about that. I know you won't understand half of those things written there. But what you are holding in your hand is a plan I want you to do…" she said, looking profoundly in his eyes. "I want you to do the same thing that the Young King and Queen did, only this time, you're going to think of Sululta as the Island," she pointed at him with her index figure, "and you're going to change everything."

Treasure breathed out in a heavy sigh, trembling. His heart beat faster. Was she really asking him to rebuild

Sululta? It seemed too big of a task for him. He felt his body becoming misty and sweaty.

"You're the saviour of this community, Young King," she said with sheer certainty.

Treasure faltered, trying to say something, his mouth gaping as though he had an impediment, struggling to get the words out, "B-But Professor, I-I can't-"

"Yes, you can!" Professor Pittman retorted in a brusque and commanding tone, like a lieutenant. "You've already done it… Haven't you taught your mother how to read? Haven't you tried and stopped your father from beating up your mother? Coming here every day to help little Lelo? Lived a life different from your peers, said no to peer pressure, remained sober and upright whilst your friends stood at that container drinking and getting high…?"

Treasure swallowed, his eyes became glassier and he felt a huge lump lodged somewhere in his throat.

"You've done it all," Professor Pittman said. "You have it in you, it takes courage and unfathomable strength to do what you're doing, to persevere like you do… If there is one person I know who can do this, it is you." She sat back on her couch, "Now go home and read through that at least three times and tell me how you're going to do it." She asked him to go and told him to take good care of the proposal and not to lose it, "It's my Treasure…," she added.

Before Treasure walked out the house, he asked Professor Pittman if he could have some of her plastic bottles.

"Sure," she assented keenly, "knock yourself out, take as much as you like."

Treasure thanked her, "Professor," he called again. She turned around, "Mr Geldof, do you think he's really going to come back?"

Professor Pittman gulped and shook her head, "I don't know Treasure," she said. "Sometimes people make promises they can't keep. But don't put your heart into it."

Treasure dropped his head, nodded and looked up again, "But the Americans… they will come right?"

Professor Pittman felt a painful lump in her throat, "I don't know son, but it's always good to believe."

Treasure gathered a couple of bottles and walked home, still stunned. He couldn't believe how Professor

Pittman could ask him to do something so big. He felt so tiny and so small, so unwise and undeserving. *Where would I even start? What would I do? How would I work with people I do not even speak to? Nobody really likes me.*

He did not feel like he could do it. Nevertheless, Professor Pittman had told him something else he never believed about himself. She told him he had a purpose and for the first time, he believed it.

6

Every minute, FIVE children died. Professor Pittman scurried through the white tents, filled to capacity, with wailing babies and crying mothers. It was a cacophony of cries in the clinics, chaos overflowing.

Vultures were ravenously circling the sky, stalking the crawling little babies, waiting for them to become little corpses on the dry, parched soil. Bad had become worse. There was nothing to feed the babies, no vitamin supplements, no nutritious foods and all the wells were running low; there was nothing.

Treasure went looking for Professor Pittman at the clinics. He had his eye stuck on the video camera, capturing everything he was seeing. His eyes welled up in tears when he saw tiny corpses of little dead bony, babies scattered on the floor like dead mosquitoes. He stopped one nurse, grabbing her arm and asked her hastily whether she'd seen Professor Pittman. The nurse pointed Professor Pittman's whereabouts in the direction of the other white tents setup as clinics.

His heart was racing, his eyes wide, "Professor Pittman, Professor Pittman," he shouted repeatedly, running and not believing his eyes.

"Treasure," Professor Pittman gasped, scolding. "You're not supposed to be here." She was walking fast with long strides and a serious countenance pervaded her face, on her way to another tent filled with sick and dying children, her stethoscope was dangling ferociously around her neck and her blue scrub flapped as the wind blew against it. "You need to get out of here right now and switch that video camera off. You cannot be here."

"Yes, Professor," Treasure said, fumbling to find the off switch of the video camera and struggling to keep up with her fast pace. "I just wanted to say I've read through the Proposal -"

They reached an open tent sealed with nets. Professor Pittman yanked the curtain open and wrapped her facemask over her mouth and nose, "Treasure, son this is not the right time," Professor Pittman said, muffled behind her mask. "I'm really busy, you can't go in here, we'll talk later, alright," she yanked the curtain closed.

Treasure darted his eyes around. It was a rush, one he'd never seen before. All the nurses and doctors were scurrying like cockroaches through the tents. There were more babies coming in, carried by crying mothers and concerned nurses; the wailing of the babies was almost unbearable.

Whilst watching all the chaos, Treasure switched on his camera again and captured everything he was seeing. With his eye still stuck on the lens, he saw a big box with Vitamin Angel written on it proffered to one of the mission doctors by a man dressed in blue UN military attire, "This is all we've got Ma'am," the man said after the doctor requested some more supplies. "I'm sorry, we can only get some in a couple of months' time."

The doctor exhaled, ripped the box apart, fished inside the box and pulled out three boxes with vaccines and some multivitamins. She ran off towards the other white tents as fast as she could, with the boxes clenched to her chest.

Treasure remembered what Professor Pittman said, that Lelo was running out of vitamin supplements. He darted rapid, mischievous and terrified glances over his shoulder, moving sneakily towards the open box. Everyone was whizzing around and no one would notice if he took just one box of multivitamins and stuck it in his bag fast enough to be noticed. He scooted closer and closer, darting his eyes around and when he thought no one was looking he snatched one box, quickly shoved it in his bag and walked out as fast as he could with long, hasty strides. One nurse saw him and shouted his name. With big eyes and a rapidly beating heart, Treasure ran as fast as he could.

***

WHILST READING AGAIN THROUGH the proposal that Professor Pittman gave him, Treasure heard someone howling from a distance, "Let me go."

When Treasure glanced up, it was Kidane pulling at a little boy called Lucky by the collar. The other boys who stood beside Kidane, whilst he shoved Lucky around, were shouting and cheering Kidane on, "Hit that little white monkey!" Lucky wrestled, trying to pull himself away from Kidane, he writhed and winced but Kidane was stronger than he was.

Treasure ran towards them with his video camera rattling in his backpack, commanding Kidane to leave Lucky alone.

Kidane laughed aloud seeing Treasure running towards him, "And what are you going to do, huh?" he groaned, entering Treasure's space. Kidane's mouth was black from smoking too much marijuana. His eyes were fire red, his hands were hard, rough and scaly. His face expressed utter nonchalance. He was a sadist by nature, who found pleasure in seeing who he could hurt. All the boys who hung around him, mirrored him and became the vermin that he was. He was a disease sucking the life out of everything and everyone. Around him, everyone thought they were tough and macho, but they didn't know that they were decomposing, decaying, deluding, degrading, demoralising, diminishing, deflowering, they were simply downgrading.

Kidane tumbled over Treasure. His height was impressive, oppressive and punitive. His shoulders stretched wide on every side. His breath always smelt of alcohol, strong and flammable like ethanol. His thoughts and actions were always ignoble and abnormal. His vices were base, out of place and smothered deep on his vile face. He scowled at Treasure in black-hearted fashion, with a devil like passion, "You think you're a tough guy huh?" he hissed with a waft of bitterness.

"LET HIM GO!" Treasure commanded, looking up at Kidane.

Kidane chuckled conceitedly glancing at his friends and beckoned Treasure with his head. Lucky was trying to pull away but Kidane had quite a firm grip on his collar.

Treasure's eyes were narrow, rigid, cold and hard, "I SAID LET HIM GO!" he snarled like a vicious lion glancing up at a vicious and soulless giant. His whole demeanour showed he was fearless. He seized Lucky with a firm clutch on his arm, "C'mon, let's go," Treasure said. Little Lucky stumbled a bit, being pulled from side to side. Treasure pulling one way and Kidane the other way.

Instead, Kidane released Lucky, snatched Treasure by his shoulder, kicked his feet from beneath him and sent him flying to the floor away from him. Kidane then jumped on top of Treasure and punched him in the face, three times, without ceasing. Blood gushed out of Treasure's nose, splattered onto his shirt in red droplets. He writhed in pain, but Treasure did not dare grunt or make a whimpering noise. He remained adamant and composed. He rose up, limping, tripping and glanced at his bag. If Kidane saw the camera in his bag, he would take it or break it.

"Let's go!" Treasure said before they could notice what was in his bag. The multivitamin box and the camera were jutting out of the bag and Treasure didn't want them to see it. Lucky stooped down to picked up his hat and tottered frightened behind Treasure.

Kidane's friends cheered him on as if he had triumphed over Treasure. As Treasure tried to stoop down to pick up the Proposal, Kidane tripped him and he fell prostrate on the solid, dry ground. Kidane then compressed his knee on Treasure's back, sneering, grunting and grinding his teeth. He was pinning Treasure's face to the ground so hard that Treasure heard a crack in his jaw, "You think you're tough?" he growled. He then stood up and kicked Treasure at the side of his already bruised ribs, "Bloody Shanqella!"

Treasure rose up again, stumbling. Lucky seized him by the arm, helping him so he could rise up. Treasure pinched his bloody nose with his two fingers, cocking his head towards heaven. Lucky stooped down, attempting to pick up the Proposal from the ground, but Kidane snatched it before Lucky could get to it.

He held it up, squinted his eyes to read and chuckled. "Pro-po-sal," he read aloud spelling out every syllable like a third grader. He croaked with a devilish chuckle. "You think you're so educated, huh? So smart? Mr Einstein," he scoffed, brandishing the stack of papers in Treasure's face.

"Give it back!" Treasure said trying to snatch the paper.

Kidane pulled away abruptly, "Nah ah… you know I can tear this up into little pieces right?"

Treasure's face grew solemn, his eyes fierce and demanding. He clenched his fist and his knuckles began to decolour to a pastel brown. But he calmed himself and pleaded, "Kidane please," he said, his voice was lower. "Professor Pittman gave that to me, it's not mine. Just give it back alright, please."

Kidane snarled liked the devil, "I don't care about Professor Pittman!" he hissed and dangled the paper in Treasure's face, "You want it, huh, you want it?" he laughed, "you really think you're smarter than everyone don't you? You think you're better than us, eh?" Before he knew it, Kidane tore the Proposal into tiny pieces and scattered it on the ground… "May this be a lesson to you!" he hissed.

Treasure's eyes gathered tears like clouds, picking up what remained of the Proposal. The ripping of the paper felt worse than the beating. He cried from the depths of his heart. He felt stripped of his treasure and shattered to pieces. What was he going to tell Professor Pittman? She strictly told him that it was her life.

***

WHEN HE GOT HOME, TREASURE threw himself on the bed and cried a muffled cry with his pillow over his face, punching the bed and kicking his feet.

What was he going to tell Professor Pittman? Why were things going sideways for him? There were so many things he wished were right and he did not know how to fix it. It was weighing heavily on him.

"Will I ever be happy?" The question lingered in his mind. The boy cried a lot, alone. As a person who always tried to help everybody, he could not help himself this time.

Even if he tried to rewrite the Proposal over, he still didn't understand what was going on. The document was typed and he had no typewriter. What was he going to do?

7

Every minute, SIX children died.

For three days, Treasure had not been to Professor Pittman's house. He experienced a rollercoaster of moods and he kept back chatting his mother. He didn't know how to stop it. He just hated his life. Suicide kept flashing like the light in an ivory tower. This kind of pain and depression was not worth enduring. Painful ulcers developed in his mouth. They increased his mood swings and made him unable to eat.

The regret would come to him in quiet moments, such as when he was going to sleep or sat alone at lunch. The only person he seemed to talk to was Lucky. Lucky always had a way to him, but his jokes were not funny.

"You're still worried about those pieces of paper aren't you?" Lucky asked.

Treasure nodded, "It's not just pieces of paper," he said, dolefully. "She trusted me with her life. She spent a lot of time writing it and I lost it."

Lucky brooded, "You know, I don't mean to add salt to your wounds, but does stressing and worrying about it make anything better?"

Treasure glanced at Lucky and away again.

"Can't you see you're losing yourself?" Lucky said. "It's just pieces of paper-"

"IT'S NOT JUST PIECES OF PAPER!" Treasure snapped.

"Well, you can't change anything now…" Lucky said. "You need to learn to change the changeable, accept the unchangeable and move on."

With some relief, Treasure lifted his eyes to Lucky, "It was her life-"

"No it wasn't," Lucky retorted. "She's still alive, isn't she?"

Treasure surged up off the bench, "Listen, this is not a joke. The Proposal meant everything to her."

Lucky stood up too and shrugged, "Well, if it really meant that much to her, then why did she give it to you?" he asked. "If she cares so much about it, she will write it again," he said shrugging and spreading his arms, "what else could you do, it wasn't your fault-"

"It was," Treasure said and sat down again. "I shouldn't have taken it with me," he slapped his forehead, gritting his teeth. "DAMMIT, how could I be so stupid?"

Lucky stared at Treasure and thought he was sabotaging himself for something he couldn't fix, "So if your house burnt down, you were going to do the same thing to yourself?"

Treasure raised his gaze, glanced at Lucky and gulped without an answer.

"Why did you take Proposal with you…?" Lucky said. "You wanted to read it right, just like she instructed you…"

Treasure looked up at Lucky again feeling a little bit more comfortable.

"Listen," Lucky added. "You did the right thing, but unfortunately, it was at the wrong time, you had no control over it and in life… in life everything happens for a reason, even the things we have no control over."

Lucky grabbed his backpack and tossed it over his shoulder, "You know," he said, jumping, his voice a little bit more melancholic. "What you're feeling is what I deal with every single day of my life. Every day, I ask myself who's going to say what about my white skin today, who's going to reject me or just dislike me. If she rejects you and hates you for what happened, at least you know where you stand. Unlike me, black inside and white on the outside…"

Treasure gulped feeling a lump lodge in his throat. All of a sudden, he felt his energy shifting towards Lucky.

"I am human…" Lucky said, "and so are you. We all make mistakes… some mistakes we can fix and some we can't… Go talk to her man," Lucky said and walked away and turned around again. "You know, you should be happy to have a friend like me. I'm a wisdom guru," he shrugged exposing his palms, "what else could I ask for, Chief!"

Lucky swaggered away to his girlfriend. When he got to her, he hugged her around her body and he flattered her, with flowery compliments and buttered her up a little. She was twice his height and twice his weight. She was a dark-skinned girl, chubby with buffy cheeks, who shadowed over him. He hugged her as a little child would hug her father, around his waist. Lucky always made her laugh, in fact he made everyone laugh and his presence was heavenly to most people he encountered.

Treasure felt like a huge weight was taken off his shoulders. He felt the raging waves in his soul go still.

Without hesitation, he got home, got undressed and made his way to Professor Pittman. He stood in front of her door and hesitated to knock. His hands were shaking convulsively. He knocked twice and he heard Professor Pittman shout from the dining room. She knew his soft knock.

She opened with a smile and a gleam on her face, then invited him in. A gesture he was not expecting, but still, he hadn't told her yet. She spoke to him as if Treasure was missing for years. She asked about his mother and school, all the matters of life, small and big. When Treasure walked inside the dining room, his eyes popped wide open when he saw Lucky sitting on the couch, with the pieces of the Proposal scattered on the table. Treasure gulped and squirmed.

Professor Pittman smiled at him tight-lipped, "Everything will be alright, my boy," Professor Pittman said, in a compassionate tone. "Lucky told me what happened." She was more relaxed and excited than she was sad. She comforted Treasure and couldn't allow him to apologise when he tried to explain himself.

"You know what," she said, "this is just an opportunity in disguise. I will teach both of you how to write, how does that sound?"

Treasure and Lucky shrugged, smiling at each other, "That sounds great, Professor," they both said in unison.

"Well then, excellent!" Professor Pittman gasped. "This might just be an opportunity for you youngsters to prove your genius," she pointed at a stack of little booklets on the table next to Treasure and summoned him to bring them to her.

Treasure pulled them out, blew the dust off them and proffered them to her.

"Ah, thank you, there you go," she said. "You see, these books will teach you everything you need to know about Youth as Agents of Behavioural Change. Everything you need to know is in here," she said tapping the covers of the books. "And everything that is in here, you can now use to write your own proposal and change the world."

Treasure and Lucky glanced at each other, with beaming eyes. Their expressions were keen. "Thank you, Professor Pittman," they said almost simultaneously.

Professor Pittman chuckled, "Don't mention it, knowledge is free. You just have to expose yourself to it. Now you boys go and read those books at least twice. Write me a small review of what you understood and we will take it from there."

The boys assented and thanked Professor Pittman. She hugged both of them in a tight bear hug and told Treasure not to worry about what had happened. No one had ever hugged them like that before. There was something so warm and comforting about Professor Pittman's embrace. They both shrank in her arms.

Treasure and Lucky could not wait to dig inside the pages. They really wanted to change the world, what else would they want. It just sounded interesting to say it; they really didn't know how to change the word, but they felt like they just had to.

The two youngsters walked out with effervescent expressions, their eyes fixed on the pictures on the front covers. They felt quite important to be given such a big task. Treasure had made himself a friend.

"Listen man," Treasure said as they walked down the road, "I just want to say thank you for what you did today… It really meant a lot to me. No one has ever done something like that for me… thank you."

Lucky stretched his clenched fist sideways, "Don't mention it, buddy," Lucky said and they bumped fists. "We're in this together. Besides, you were there for me as well. The greatest gift of life is a true friend and I have received one," he said and shrugged exposing his palms, "What else could I ask for, Chief! I'm blessed. I am fire walking, about to change the world… I'm gonna set myself ablaze and the world will come watch me burn, just watch me."

Treasure laughed and threw his arms over Lucky's shoulders, "When Mr Geldof comes back and the Americans come here with BIG aeroplanes, we will be ready."

This was the beginning of the life and the start of a new friendship, filled with an abundance of opportunities. The two Young Kings had begun to share the same dream, ambition and goal. They had a common interest, changing the world. What else could bind a friendship as tightly and relentlessly as a noble pursuit? How would they change the world?

8

Every minute, SEVEN children died.

Treasure was wondering around amongst the gaunt, scrawny cows feeding near the dry riverbank. The mooing of the cows were tired and weary. He was carrying an *insera* (a clay container) and filling it with the little dung that the cows excreted onto the ground, stuffing it up with his hands and shoving it into the container. It was warm, mushy and somewhat smelly too but he was used to the smell because his mother used to mix it with soil and water, then smear the dung onto the floor to preserve it.

Whilst Treasure stood bent over, scooping up a handful of cow dung with his nose crinkled and his face screwed up in a grimace, he heard a heavy DOOM sound coming from behind him. He turned around abruptly and saw a scrawny cow dropping to the ground. He leapt up hastily onto his feet, ran to the cow and dropped onto his knees next to it. The poor cow was gasping and her moo was abnormal. She was suffocating, saliva dribbled out of her mouth, with her tongue hanging aimlessly to the side - the cow was dying.

Treasure hastily leapt up again, scurried to his basin, scooped a handful of dung and ran back to the cow. He felt a lump lodged in his throat as he tried to stuff the dung into its mouth, feeding it, "ssshh," he hissed, quietening the cow brushing its head, "irefiti," he whispered repeatedly in a soft, gentle tone, "irefiti." Irefiti means sleep in Amharic.

The cow wiggled her tongue around trying to scoop the dung into her mouth and chew but she had little energy in her. Treasure squirted a bit of water from his little leather water bag into her mouth, but it was too late. Slowly the mooing of the cow became softer, softer and softer – then it was dead quiet.

It was unsightly for Treasure and brought him into a gloomy state, but the Young King was as tough as nails. With tears in his eyes and a painful lump in his throat, Treasure exhaled aloud, "Beselami ārifewali," he said. This meant, rest in peace. He started milking the cow, squirting the milk inside his leather water bag. When he was done, he gathered his clay container and started walking back home. When he turned his head back once more, he saw the little calves moving towards the dead mother and starting to feed on her. Do they even know they will never see their mother again? He thought and continued walking downcast, his body slumped over, his heart heavy and he felt all the more that he needed to do something, but he didn't know what.

When he reached home, he went to the garden and started cutting some of the bottles that Professor Pittman gave him. He cut the bottles in half in the middle, filled the bottom half with some water, took some wick material, wet the wick and placed it through the bottle mouth down to the water. He mixed some of the cow dung with some leaves, dry grass clippings and weeds, using a pitchfork.

Whilst caught up in his duties, still distraught and sombre because of what he saw today, he didn't notice that his mother was standing behind him with her hands on her hips and a curious crinkle on her forehead, "what are you doing?" she asked.

Treasure jumped and flinched, wide-eyed, "Imayē," he gasped, winded, "you scared me… I'm making some compost."

"What for? We've already planted the seeds in the soil," she said. "We can't dig them out again-"

"I know," Treasure retorted.

"And what are you going to do with those," she said pointing at the scattered bottles on the ground.

Treasure picked up the bottle, "These…? I want to try something," he said shrugging. "Just an idea I have."

His mother smiled, squinting her eyes wondering what he was now up to, "Mmm, I'm curious… would you mind sharing?"

Treasure wavered because he doubted that it would work; he didn't want to share with her, but he thought he would anyway, "I want to grow kale in these containers," fumbling with the top half of the cut bottle.

His mother frowned, her mouth pursed but slightly open and loose. Her eyes were fixed as if she was looking at something a yard behind Treasure's head, "How can you grow kale in those containers?" she said. "Kale needs to be grown in water and soil? Like all other vegetables."

"I know," Treasure said, "but we have no water and we have no rain, so the kale won't grow…" he picked up one bottle, "but if there's an endless water supply… It will work the same way a kerosene lamp works, the wick will draw water to the seed and the kale will grow. "

His mother was still disconcerted and she exhaled, smiling, thinking her son was just playing around.

"I know it sounds silly," he said and picked up the wick, "Professor Pittman told me that fabric can suck up water, like it sucks up paraffin. So, if I put this, amidst the seeds and the compost, the kale will grow."

His mother exhaled, smiled and nodded, not sure herself that it would work, "Do it and let's see if it works," she said and told him she had to finish cleaning the house, but she couldn't wait to see what happened.

Treasure smiled confidently tight-lipped and twitched an eyebrow at her.

He soaked the wick and filled the bottom half of the bottle with water, stuffed some of the wet wick through the mouth of the bottle and dropped some of the wick to the water at the bottom. He filled the top half with the compost mixture, compressed it in the bottom half of the bottle and stuffed in some kale seeds, making sure the seeds were very close to the wick.

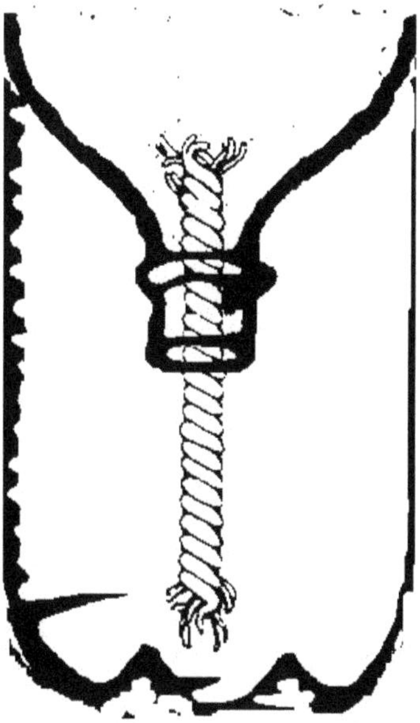

He picked up the bottle gingerly, took it to his room and placed it on top of his tattered and raggedy bedside table made of sticks. If this seed would grow, he would be able to grow the kale at school, teach the other kids how to do it and there would be food again in the whole of Sululta.

Treasure stuffed his video camera into his bag, looking around making sure that no one saw him with it. He didn't even want his mother to know that he had it, because if his father discovered it, he would take it, sell it and buy alcohol with the money. So, he couldn't risk that.

Treasure had a plan. He still had that salty taste of sweat in his mouth and smelt of cow dung but he didn't care. He had an idea bubbling inside of him. He walked to Lucky's house in brisk hasty steps, his feet scratching feet on the rough ground, mumbling to himself, "If the Americans would see the video, they would come and help us, like Professor Pittman… all I need to do is to get this video to them." His head was buzzing with ideas of how he could save the dying children and stop the famine. He didn't know exactly how he could get it to rain, but he knew he could find a way to save the children.

The wind blew through the branchy trees, blowing dust in the air and sand in Treasure's eyes. If the rain didn't come, Sululta would turn into a desert, more people would die and Treasure would never make it to medical school and become a doctor like Professor Pittman. He would not be able to save millions of lives and build his mother a BIG house with a beautiful green garden, which was all he wanted.

Lucky lived with his mother in a two bedroom mud brick house with a rusted iron roof. Although the house was raggedy, it looked fairly better than Treasure's house.

Treasure shouted Lucky's name when he got closer to the house. Lucky hollered back, sitting with his knees on a huge stone that overlooked their village. He called this stone, his royal stone. Nobody else sat there but him.

"You should stop shouting my name like that," Lucky said, "you're just reminding God who to kill next."

Treasure chuckled perching himself next to him, "I've got something to show you," Treasure said and looked around, "but you can't tell anyone about it."

Lucky stared at him, listening attentively.

Treasure rummaged in his bag and pulled out the video camera. Lucky's eyes became round and big, "Where did you-"

"Ssshh," Treasure shushed him.

"Where did you get that?" Lucky said, whispering.

Treasure smiled, "Professor Pittman, she gave it to me for my birthday."

Lucky's heart was pulsating; he only saw these from people who came to their village, with big vans and trucks, "Have you used it?"

Treasure nodded, "Yeah, I went to the clinic and took some videos."

Lucky frowned, dumbfounded, "Why the clinic?"

Treasure exhaled, "I have an idea."

"About what?"

Treasure paused a while looking at the mountains and the horizon, "I want to take a video, then send it to the Americans and they will come to help us."

Lucky frowned, as though he was disgusted. He really didn't understand what Treasure was saying. "I don't understand?"

Treasure wavered and exhaled aloud trying to find a way to explain it to Lucky, "Look if, I can take videos of how the children are dying, how little food we have and send it to the Americans, they will come like Professor Pittman to help us."

Lucky still didn't understand how that would work, in fact he thought it was stupid, he chuckled, "You're crazy man, do you really think they will come here and help us just because some boy sent them a video of poor people and dying babies, do you think they care about that? I mean how would you even get it there? Do you even know how it works," Lucky said pointing at the camera, "you don't have a TV and a video player."

Treasure brooded for a minute and then lifted up the camera, "I read the instructions," he dug into his bag and pulled out a little paper and started explaining to Lucky how to know when the video camera was recording, explaining to him that a red light beams when the camera was recording. He pulled out the video tape and lifted it to the sky, "You see, this side which is still the smallest circle is everything I recorded and this side with the biggest circle is the side I still have left for recording."

Lucky nodded, "Okay, I understand, but how will you get that to the Americans?"

Treasure brooded and a light beamed, "Professor Pittman, she always receives letters from friends in America, she gets them through the United Nations Military postal services."

Lucky nodded again, "Ok, but this is not a letter, it's a video tape. What if you lose it or it doesn't get there?"

Treasure thought about it for a while. Lucky was right, he only had one tape to record.

"And who exactly are you sending it to?" Lucky added.

Treasure shrugged, "I don't know, but I can find out. We can't sit here and do nothing. We need some more people to help us." He thought of Lelo. "Can you imagine how many children we can save if more doctors like Professor Pittman could come and help us?"

Lucky was doubtful that it would work, but he didn't want to let Treasure know that he didn't think it was a good idea. "Look man, nobody has time for us. Not everybody is like Professor Pittman. Nobody would leave their country to come live in a country where nothing lives-"

"Yes, I know," Treasure retorted, with gusto. "They don't have to live here, even if they come for a day, a week or a month, I don't know, it doesn't matter. But they can teach us or some of us and then we can use what they teach us to help the children."

Lucky began to think that it made sense, but he still couldn't see how that was possible and how Treasure would even achieve something like that. Lucky exhaled and stood up on the rock, "Well, whatever, you want, I will help you," he said, spreading his arm, "but, I still don't think it's smart to send them the ONLY video tape you have."

They paused for a moment brooding, "I can send them letters," Treasure murmured.

Lucky stared at him.

Treasure leapt up blissfully, "Yes, I can send them letters. I-I can write to them and - and tell them how much we're struggling and suffering and they must bring their big aeroplanes to help us."

Lucky shook his head, downcast, "It won't work, Treasure."

"It will!" Treasure retorted. "C'mon you gotta help me with this, please," he begged clenching his hands, "please, you'll never know, maybe they'll even write back to us and when they write back to us, then we will send them the video tape and show them everything that is happening."

Lucky nodded, deciding to play the passive role and acquiesce, "Okay, suppose they come here, what will they teach us? We're not doctors, you remember what

Professor Pittman told us, it took her eleven years to become a specialist. Eleven years… we don't have so much time, we need something now and fast."

For the first time, Treasure told someone about what he did after school. He told Lucky about Lelo and how Professor Pittman taught him how to take care of Lelo, he told him how she taught him to caregive for her, bed wash her, measure the medicine doses, nutrition and hygiene. "Could you imagine what will happen if more doctors would come and teach more of us that? Help other's using their gifts." Treasure picked up a stick and drew on the ground. "If one doctor teaches ten people of Sululta the same things that Professor Pittman teaches me, that one person can save ten babies. If ten doctors teach ten people, we would have a hundred skilled people who are able to save babies lives… How many babies will be saved?"

Lucky now had an enlightened smile on his face. "A thousand babies can be saved by one hundred caregivers," Lucky murmured, a little bit less arrogant because everything was making sense.

"Yes," Treasure shrieked, "so all we need is ten doctors, to share their gifts with us. And we do the same, using our gifts, no matter how small they are."

Lucky nodded, but there were still some doubts in his mind, "Treasure, the government is probably already busy doing something, let's just wait and see-"

"I WILL NOT WAIT," Treasure snapped, "I am not a chained citizen waiting for the state to look after me, I want to take the risk, to strive and to build; I'm willing to fail in order to succeed, but waiting," he shook his head, "nah, I'm not gonna wait man. I'm gonna do it… you only live once, my friend, only once… People and children are dying don't you get that? The government is too busy talking, what we need to do is to just do it… and when the Americans come, they will meet us half way, all we need to do is to start. Our efforts can help improve the lives of children in Sululta, maybe even the whole of Ethiopia." Treasure raised his hands, "Who knows, maybe the entire world… Every child deserves a safe and happy childhood. But there are still millions of children in Ethiopia who grow up without the basics and we need to make sure they get the basics. So are you in or are you out, but either way, I'm willing to do it without you?" Treasure said with a serious face. Treasure spoke with sheer gusto and passion.

Lucky could feel the adrenalin surging through his body. His breathing became shallower and his eyes wider. Lucky smiled and his lips began to spread broader and broader, "Of course, I'm in," Lucky said nodding and looked at the drawing on the ground, "but I'll have to teach you how to draw first."

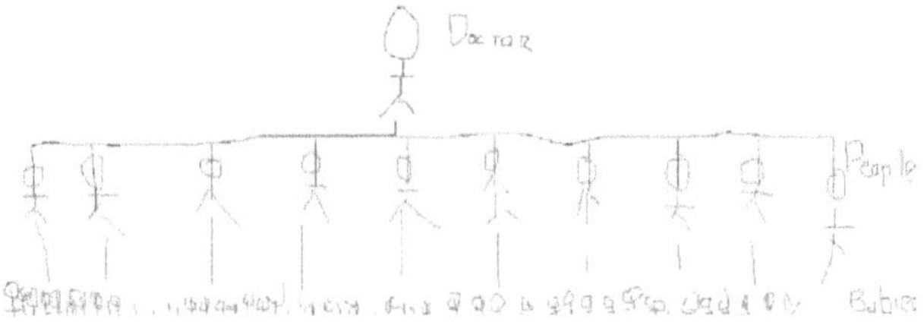

Treasure laughed and muzzled his head and threw his arms over Lucky's shoulders, "You know what this is called?" Lucky asked.

"What?"

"It's called Pass it Forward," Lucky said. "The networking of good deeds. Which means the recipient of the favour does a favour for ten others. However, it needs to be a BIG favour that the receiver can't complete themselves… However, it needs to be a favour where one can use their gifts to change someone or the world."

Treasure nodded, "Wow, you explain it better than I do."

Lucky chuckled pompously, "That's because I'm a genius!"

Treasure mussed his head and threw his arms over him. The Young Kings were ready.

9

Heat showered down upon Lucky and Treasure like a gust from hell. The singed sand glistened in the fierce white rays of the sun. Their hats enveloped their heads in warm salty sweat and the dry heat singed their lungs. Nothing and no one moved in this penetrating heat, unless they were desperate and they were.

Their stomachs growled and rumbled as they approached the Save the Children Feeding Centre. They weren't talking and Treasure had his eye focussed on his video camera. This somehow took his attention away from the hole in his stomach.

Lucky's pale skin was red, sweat trickled down his face and arms. He wiped his forehead with his arm, "You're going to finish that tape, by recording everything you see," Lucky said, whilst kicking some stones on the ground.

Treasure didn't respond and had his camera set to a vulture soaring over a particular tree. His breathing was rapid, "Look, a vulture!"

Lucky darted his eyes towards the horizon, squinting his eyes, "They're everywhere man, you don't have to take videos of birds."

Treasure ignored him and all of a sudden, Treasure surged ahead, started running, shouting at the vulture that just landed on the ground trying to scare it away, flailing his arms and running as fast as he could.

Lucky called on him wondering what he was seeing, but Treasure ran faster and faster shouting at the vulture. When they were closer, the vulture flapped, flapped and flew away. There was a little girl like next to where the vulture had landed at the trail leading to the Feeding Centre. The little girl was gaunt with scrawny legs and ribs poking out of her stomach. She had collapsed, weakened from hunger.

Lucky and Treasure stood, eyes wide with their hands on their heads. They looked around and perhaps thought there might be a parent nearby but there was nothing.

Treasure untangled his video camera, gave it to Lucky and stooped down, next to the little girl. He felt her pulse which was still beating slowly. He turned the little girl over and laid her flat on the ground; he placed his ear next to her chest and check for breathing, looked for chest movement, listened for breath sounds and felt for breathing movements. She was still breathing but she wasn't breathing normally, "Quickly," he said to Lucky, "run and call for help."

Lucky nodded and ran shouting for help, flailing his hands. The Feeding Centre was just fifty metres away.

Treasure placed his hands in the centre of her chest and using the heel of his palm, pushed hard and fast. He remembered what Professor Pittman taught him, to push at a rate of 100 compressions a minute, 5cm deep. He placed his face near her cheeks to check if he could hear or feel breath, then looked along her chest to see if her breath was rising and falling, the girl was breathing again.

He took some of his water from his water pouch and poured a little slowly into her mouth and gently dripped the milk, he had milked from the cow and squirted the little that came out into her mouth, "Met'et'i," he said to her gently rubbing her head telling her to drink, "met'et'i." When he lifted his eyes, he saw Lucky running back with two nurses carrying a stretcher.

Treasure stood up and gave the nurses some room. "She's still breathing," he said.

One of the nurses stooped down and pressed her stethoscope to the little girl's chest, listening for her heartbeat, "She's breathing," she said and pulled on the little girl's eyes. Her pupils were dilated, her eyes were white and full of tears. The little girl had no strength to cry out.

The nurses assembled the little girl, picked her up and rested her on the stretcher, looked for a vein and inserted the butterfly needle with a plastic tube attached to the bag of sterile fluids. The other nurse held the colourless bag filled with a watery liquid high enough so that the solution ran down through the tube, while they walked back to the Feeding Centre, with Treasure carrying the head end of the stretcher, one nurse carrying the foot end and the other one holding the bag in the air.

"What is it that you put into her arm?" Lucky asked the nurse,

"Saline fluid," Treasure retorted, "the drip will allow the fluid to go directly into a vein quickly."

Lucky looked at the nurse carrying the bag to validate what Treasure just said.

The nurse was impressed, she beamed a little smirk, "You're right," she said. "Where did you learn that from?"

"Professor Pittman," Treasure said, "she teaches me every day after school."

The nurse nodded, "You boys did an amazing job with the girl and if it wasn't for you… she would have died. Well done, you saved her life."

Treasure felt his heart swell up and a huge lump lodged in his throat, "Where was she going to?" Treasure asked.

The nurse exhaled aloud, with tears in her eyes, "She's hungry and she wants food."

Treasure and Lucky looked at each other. They too were coming for food and some more videos.

After the little girl received attention from the doctors, Lucky and Treasure sat feeling profoundly distressed on a large timber log, eating bread and soup.

Lucky sighed like a slight spring breeze, softly and gently, "What are we going to do, man?" he asked. "It seems to be getting worse. Why don't they take every child in the villages and bring them here?"

Treasure shook his head, downcast, "It won't make any difference. There isn't enough food and medicine… They'll still die."

They brooded in silence for a while then Treasure stood up and stuck a few slices of bread into his bag, "Come on, let's go."

"Where are we going?" Lucky asked, standing up and following Treasure who was walking in long strides.

"We have to write that letter and send it today."

They walked back to Lucky's house distraught and troubled. Will it even work? Who were they to address the letter to?

"The nurses," Lucky said as they strutted down the trail.

"What about them?" Treasure said.

"They were talking about you, they said you're gifted."

Treasure glanced at him, "Well, I'm not, it's not like I was born with it."

Lucky paused for a moment thinking of whether he should tell him what else they said, "They – they also talked about Professor Pittman."

"Everybody knows Professor Pittman," Treasure retorted, somewhat exasperated. It was hot and he didn't want to talk.

"Yeah, I know but…" Lucky said and exhaled. "They said she can get into real trouble if she continued teaching you."

Treasure stopped abruptly, "What?"

Lucky sighed and looked away.

"Lucky, what did they say?" Treasure asked, grabbing his shoulder.

He brooded and scratched his head, "They said it was against the organisation's policy. If anybody would find out… they'd fire her."

Treasure brooded, "But Professor Pittman is a university qualified Professor and she also teaches biology-"

"She's not supposed to be teaching you how to work on a human body," Lucky said. "She needs clearance from her organisation for that."

"But we saved that little child!" Treasure said, frustrated, pointing towards where they had found her. "She could have died, they said so themselves."

"Yeah, but-"

"But what?" Treasure shrilled, his face glittering with sweat and fury. "Don't pay too much attention to what people are saying, we saved that child's life and that's all that matters. We need more help, so we can save more children," he said and walked off briskly.

"Treasure, we are not doctors or nurses," Lucky said, frustrated. "We're just grade twelve scholars, we can't save these kids."

Treasure turned around and towered over Lucky, "Listen!" he shouted. "I don't care what they say, or what anybody says. The kids are dying, we're hungry. If they're not helping us, we are going to do it ourselves and when Mr Geldof comes back, he will see what we've done. And the Americans are coming too. They will come here with BIG aeroplanes, bringing us food."

Lucky spoke with his head to the dusty ground, "Nobody is coming Treasure," he said dolefully. "It's been over five months now. I – I just think we should take it slow-"

"RUBBISH!" Treasure snapped. "A child almost died in front of us, this morning a cow died right in front of my eyes. Every day, little babies die... Now it's either you're with me or I'm going to do this alone..." Treasure waited for an answer.

Lucky faltered, not knowing what to say. He was afraid and couldn't look Treasure in the eyes. He thought Treasure was too deep in it.

Treasure could tell by Lucky's silence that he didn't want to do it, "You know what," Treasure said after a pause. "FINE," Treasure hissed. "If you're not in, I'll do this on my own. You're just like the others... weak. And for your information... Mr Geldof and the Americans WILL come," he said and walked away in brisk strides.

Lucky's lower lip quivered as the words slowly made their way out of his mouth, "Treasure wait..." he mumbled with his body slumping, but Treasure continued walking, hammering the ground with long, heavy strides until he disappeared from sight.

10

Treasure was at Professor Pittman's house, as she took him through their daily processes. Little Lelo was getting better. Her hair was slowly growing back again and her body was getting fuller.

"She's recovering quite well," Professor Pittman said.

Treasure nodded and didn't respond. He had been quiet the whole day and not very responsive.

Professor Pittman peered at him, "Treasure are you okay? You've been very quiet," she said snapping off her latex gloves.

Treasure nodded, "Yeah, I'm fine, just tired."

She walked closer to him and touched his shoulder, "You know, you can talk to me about anything?"

Treasure gulped and nodded. He didn't want to tell her about what happened the day before. He remembered that she had warned him before not to let anyone know about what she was teaching him.

"Pack up," Professor Pittman said, "I'll be in the kitchen."

Treasure nodded, "Professor," he called before she walked out the door.

Professor Pittman turned around, "Yeah?"

"What would happen if someone found out what you're teaching me?"

Professor Pittman peered at him, scrutinising him closely, "They'll probably fire me… why? Did you tell someone?"

"No – No, no one," Treasure said shaking his head rapidly, stammering.

Professor Pittman looked at him with eyes of suspicion and nodded, "Make sure you close the windows, there's a lot of mosquitoes… and leave the door open."

Treasure nodded and waited until she was out of sight. Treasure quickly stooped down to his backpack, taking out the multivitamin he had taken from the clinic. He crushed it into little fine pieces so Lelo would be able to swallow them. He speared another quick glance at the door, popping open the multivitamin liquid, removed the feeding bottle from her mouth, poured in some of the multivitamin syrup, wiped her mouth, stuffed the bottle back in her mouth and quickly stuck the syrup back in his backpack.

He walked out looking innocent and Professor Pittman was in the kitchen pouring some tea.

"I – I have to go now, bye" Treasure said.

"Wait, are you leaving without having some tea?" she squeaked. "Have something to eat first."

"No – No, I'm fine," Treasure said then walked to the door and said he would see her the next day. He turned around abruptly at the door again. "Professor," he said. "Have you heard anything from Geldof?"

Professor Pittman gulped, she had lost all hope that Bob Geldof would return, but she didn't want to break his heart. He was just a boy with a dream, but she still wished to tell him to get it all out of his mind. She shook her head, "No, nothing."

"Not even the news?" Treasure said.

"…Not even the news, Treasure."

Treasure brooded and nodded, "But the Americans will come, Professor," Treasure said positively and nodded, "You will see… They will come here with BIG aeroplanes bringing us food and Michael Jackson will be there too, you will be here to see that, right?"

Professor Pittman nodded, teary eyed, "I will always be here son, always."

Treasure smiled even more broadly, "Well, thank you Professor, I'll see you tomorrow." He walked out of the door before Professor Pittman could say bye.

Professor Pittman stood in the kitchen frozen and gobsmacked, shook her head and went to the dining room.

***

ON HIS WAY BACK, just in front of his gate, at his house, Lucky was sitting down waiting for him. When he got closer, Lucky stood up dusting the sand off his pants and greeted him.

"Hi," Treasure retorted shortly and crossed his arms, with his face tense.

"Listen," Lucky started, "I'm sorry about yesterday. I didn't mean to make you angry."

Treasure tightened his jaw and looked away, "It's fine," he said. "I shouldn't have yelled at you like that and besides, you were right. Professor Pittman could get into big trouble if they find out, she told me."

Lucky's eyes widened, "Did you tell her?"

Treasure shook his head, "No, I just couldn't. After all she has done for me... how can I be so stupid!"

Lucky exhaled, "If it works... they won't fire her."

Treasure glanced at Lucky, "if what works?"

Lucky smiled, "That idea you proposed to me. If we get Professor Pittman to teach ten of us... we can help save the children."

Treasure smiled back, "so you're in?"

Lucky nodded, "I wouldn't let you do it alone, man."

Treasure smiled even more broadly, "Thank you, I appreciate it."

Lucky flicked an eyebrow, "So, where do we start?"

Treasure exhaled, "We need to start writing those letters, send those videos and then we need to get Professor Pittman to teach us."

Lucky chuckled, "We both know that won't work and we both can't write to save our lives..." he looked at

Treasure intensely. "I have a better idea… you teach us and we both know who's the best writer in the school."

They both looked at each other, Treasure frowned, "Who? Simone?" he squeaked.

"Yep," Lucky said, nodding. "She's the only one-"

"Hell no!" Treasure barked. "I've never even spoken to her."

Lucky shrugged and began backing away, "We have no other choice."

"And how am I going to teach and who's going to ask her?"

Lucky smiled and pointed at Treasure with both his index fingers, "You will… You are going to teach us the same way you saved the little girl," Lucky said and raised a salute, "cheers man, see you tomorrow."

Treasure faltered and wavered. His heart beating rapidly. How was he going to teach them? Where and with what? In addition to that, how was he going to speak to that weird girl, Simone?

11

Treasure pressed his slender fingers into the skin of his forearms, his nails penetrating the layer of fine dust. His whole body shook, his bones rattled in constant fear of speaking to a girl.

When he saw Simone leaving the school gate, his heart vaulted so hard against his ribcage as his pulse pressed outward, jerking the veins within, "Si-Simone," he said, stammering.

Simone turned around and when she saw it was Treasure, even her heart leaped to her throat, her eyes beamed open, "Hi-Hi," she said stammering, folding her arms and looking down.

"M-May I talk to you for a moment?"

Simone looked around, wavering, her mouth gaping open, "I-I," she stammered and cleared her throat, "I have to get home."

"It's fine, I'll talk while we walk."

Simone gulped swallowing, her heart even beating much faster, “Okay,” she croaked and stroked her braids behind her ear, wondering what Treasure would want to say to her. He had never spoken to her.

They walked down the dusty road with a short surge of nervous silence. Treasure cleared his throat, “Listen, I know this is weird of me coming to you like this.”

Simone swallowed and blinked at Treasure, listening attentively.

“But I need, well WE need your help,” Treasure said.

She looked back up at him; a gentle flush of pink twinkled on her cheeks that made her look vulnerable. Why would Treasure need help from her? “Help with what?” she timidly asked.

Treasure exhaled, “Well, there’s something Lucky and I would like to do… I know it might sound weird, but… we want the Americans to come and help us, like Professor Pittman. And I spoke to Mr Geldof… the one who came to our school remember? He said he would come back to help us, so when he comes, we will be ready,” he said.

Simone nodded with a frown, halting her strides, "But I'm not sure I understand."

Treasure brooded, "How do I put it… Okay, we want to save the children dying in our communities and we want to get more Americans, like Professor Pittman, to come to help us save more babies."

He had gotten her attention, but she still wondered how she would fit into the picture, "And what do you need me for?"

"Well," Treasure said. "We need someone who's good at writing, we want to write a letter to the Americans, tell them what we want and that we need help…" he looked at her in her eyes, "and that's why I came to you… You are the best writer in the whole school… I know it's kind of confusing, but really, if it works, we can save over one thousand children…" Treasure trailed off explaining to her how it would work. "So all we need is ten doctors, to train ten people as community health workers. If ten community health workers help ten children, that's a thousand children who will receive medical attention…"

Simone was in awe and inspired. She felt a twinkle in her heart. He really is smart, she thought. They stared back at each other for what seemed like five seconds until she finally dropped her gaze, "I'd love to be a part of that, Treasure," her voice was quieter now. She looked back up at him; a gentle smile spread across her face. "And, I'd love to help you." Simone had never much noticed Treasure before, the way she did when he told her the brilliant idea. Her eyes stayed locked on him. Her heart was somersaulting and with Treasure standing so dangerously close to her, she felt weird.

Treasure's eyes lit up and a million new ideas were streaming through his brain, "Great, we meet at Lucky's house on Saturdays and sometimes we meet at Professor Pittman's house every Wednesday afternoon."

Simone nodded with a tight-lipped smile, "Okay, I'll be there," she said, backing off. "And thanks for the invitation."

"No, thank you," Treasure said.

Simone shifted her head to one side, the dimples on the corners of her cheeks indented, "Bye, Treasure," she said and walked away, sashaying her hips a little more than usual. She glanced once more behind her and Treasure was still watching her walk away. Inside she was galloping like a pony.

Treasure saw something he had never seen about her. She was very beautiful and she was not as aloof as he thought she was.

***

WHEN TREASURE walked inside his dining room, his face fell immediately when he saw his mother, perched on the tattered sofa, "Imayē," he gasped, wide-eyed. "What happened?"

His mother had bruises everywhere on her body. Broken nails, bashed in eyes, a battered face and bloody tears. Mrs Wedu could not hold her tears back and she wept.

Treasure knew that it was his father. He heard him rumbling in his room and Treasure flew to him burning with rage. He banged his bedroom door open and the house rattled. His mother wailed at him, telling him not to go to him. Treasure found his father, swaying back and forth in his bedroom. Everything was upside down, his bed pushed against the wall, his wardrobe of cardboard racked to pieces. Treasure wandered his eyes, breathing heavy, the blood was racing in his veins, he felt his fist clench harder as he saw the mess in his bedroom. The man stood there slumbering and swaying out of balance, he looked like a toddler enlarged to adult size, exasperated in his rage, a sort of impulsiveness.

Mr Wedu stumbled forward, "Where's the money," he barked. "You hiding money from me?"

Anger boiled deep in Treasure's system, as hot as lava, "We have no money," Treasure hissed, his nostrils flared and eyes wolfish. He pointed to the door, "Get out of my room!" Treasure was trembling.

Fires of fury and hatred seethed in Mr Wedu's small red narrowed eyes, the whole house smelt like a brewery. There was silence on both sides. If hatred was visible, the air would have been blood red.

Mrs Wedu walked in and pulled Treasure by the arm, "Boy, run and go to Professor Pittman's house."

Treasure yanked his arm, "I'M NOT GOING ANYWHERE," he barked, clenching his fist and protruding his chest.

His mother begged him, but Treasure was ready to fight.

Mr Wedu sneered an impetuous laugh, "Do you want to fight me, little boy, err," he hissed, his jaw clenched and he tumbled over Treasure.

"I SAID GET OUT and leave my mother alone," Treasure growled motioning with his hand.

Mr Wedu chuckled oozing with conceitedness tossing his head backwards, blazing with arrogance, "Your mother uh… who told you she's your mother?"

"Son," Mrs Wedu said, moving in front of Treasure blocking him with her body like a dove sheltering her little ones with her wings. "Please go to Professor Pittman's house, please."

"NO, I'm sick of him," Treasure cried with spit splatting out of his mouth and veins popping from his neck and forehead. "He's an animal."

Mr Wedu was a ticking time bomb. His temper blew. He smacked her face open handed, leaving a red welt on her cheeks that showed through her darkish skin and sent Mrs Wedu flying against the wall. The slap was as loud as a clap and stung her face. Just beneath her eye was a tiny opening in the skin where the ring cut her. She clutched her face, eyes watering and sobbing.

He leapt to Treasure and struck a solid upper cut to Treasure's jaw and pinned him down with his knee, "Do you think you can fight me? huh?" he snarled, pressing Treasure harder to the ground.

"Leave him alone," Mrs Wedu cried, trying to hoist herself up, wincing in pain. She crawled and grabbed Mr Wedu's foot and he kicked her away sending her back against the wall. Treasure tried to wrestle him, but he was stronger than he was. He only stopped hitting Treasure when he saw that his teeth filled with blood.

He walked over them as if they were trash on the floor, growling, groaning, taunting and uttering slanderous remarks. "…I'm teaching you a lesson," he said and tapped his chest with his index finger, "I'm the man of this house, I'm the man here, not you," he said, kicking Treasure once more on his leg and then stumbled out the room.

Mrs Wedu crawled towards Treasure, embraced him, holding him tight, whimpering. Treasure was so used to the beating that he could not cry long about it, he looked over his mother's shoulders and his eyes reflected the stories of his pain. He glanced at the floor. At least his father had not opened his bag where the camera was. However, his father had smacked the table so hard, that it smacked his little bottle gardening project, which had scattered on the floor. As Treasure peered closer, he saw that the seed had roots… It was growing, his experiment worked.

12

When Treasure showed up at Lucky's house the next morning, Lucky felt his heart sink into a deep abyss of pain, but he never asked what happened. Everyone in the village knew that Treasure was his father's punching bag, "It worked!" Treasure exclaimed, without even greeting Lucky.

Lucky frowned, "What worked?"

"I started a gardening project to see if I could grow kale in this bottle," he said, bubbling with excitement. He pulled out the seed with its roots, "Look, it worked." Treasure, as a rule, always concealed his emotions; he tried to maintain a blank face all the time. However, that day was different. He wasn't hiding anything, he was really excited. He glowed from within, which permeated externally. The smile on his face hadn't been seen since boyhood. On their way to Professor Pittman's house, he walked faster and talked faster, with even more passion and confidence. He just had a great feeling about the day, nothing that felt this right could possibly go wrong. It just couldn't.

"Do you know what we could do at our schools if we got all the bottles and planted these in all the households, schools, hospitals… as many as we can," he said and whooped, pumping his fist in the air while jumping. "Gosh, this would be so awesome! No child would die of malnutrition."

Lucky smiled, peering at the excitement he saw in Treasure, "You know, at first I didn't believe in this, but now I do, I really do."

Treasure threw his arm over Lucky, "Don't worry, everything will work out well, even Simone said she'll write the letter."

Luck receded, startled and wide-eyed. They even stopped walking, "Wait wait, let me get this straight, Simone… the weird girl, who never talks to ANYBODY except herself said YES?"

"Uh huh," Treasure said, nodding. "Not only yes, she also said she wanted to be part of the project."

Lucky gaped in awe, as though a chicken had given birth to a pony, "Oh no, I really didn't think she'd say yes. Things are really weird."

Treasure chuckled, "She's not that bad, I also thought she wouldn't say yes."

They reached Professor Pittman's house and she was in her garden, sitting on a bucket, reading.

"Professor Pittman," Treasure greeted.

"Boys, how are you? What brings you here so early?" she asked, looking with a curious frown at what Treasure had in his hand.

Treasure and Lucky glanced at each other and Lucky beckoned with his head for him to tell her.

"Well," Treasure started. "The other day you explained to me how the paraffin worked, with the wick and the paraffin."

"Yeah," Professor Pittman drawled hungry to hear more.

"I went and tried to do it at home," Treasure said. "But only… I tried to plant kale and grow the seed," he motioned to the seed that had begun to grow roots. "Look, it worked. The seed is growing."

Professor Pittman took the seed and turned it in her hand a couple of times. Her breathing was heavier, she was stunned and she leapt onto her feet. "Wait, so you grew this in that bottle?"

"Yes, Professor."

Professor Pittman peered at both Treasure and Lucky, she could believe how it was possible.

Lucky nodded, "He really did, Professor."

Professor Pittman shook her head, "Treasure do you know what a breakthrough this would be to Sululta?"

Treasure smiled at Lucky and nodded, "Yes, Professor, actually Lucky and I are thinking of growing it in all the schools, churches and homes around Sululta."

Professor Pittman chuckled, shaking her head, "I was right!" she said. "There is something about you. Nobody else would have thought about this, except you, Treasure."

Treasure smiled, downcast, "Thank you, Professor… we also have someone else joining us…"

Lucky cleared his throat, "Speak of the devil."

Treasure looked behind him when he heard footsteps cracking on the ground. It was Simone, who followed them.

Simone greeted them.

"Simone," Treasure said. "I was just telling Professor Pittman that you decided to join us."

Professor Pittman felt a nervous energy flow through her body. On the other hand, it was inspiring and great to witness. She knew she had done it. All she needed was someone to agree and there they were, two Kings and a Queen ready to change the world.

***

FOR THE next couple of weeks, The Young Kings and Queen gathered as many bottles as they could find. Sometimes they walked miles and miles to the UN Military camps looking for empty bottles and hiked to Addis Ababa. Sometimes Professor Pittman helped them. They gathered as many as two thousand coke bottles and Professor Pittman even got some imported. Treasure trained Lucky and Simone on how to plant. However, they needed more volunteers and Lucky made this his duty; since what he was good at, once he got someone's attention, was that he could get them to do anything he wanted.

They had mobilised themselves into three support structures. Treasure was the Brain (teacher and planner), Lucky was the Mouth (recruiter and speaker) and Simone was the Hands (writer and organiser). They used exactly the same methods that the Young King and Queen did in the story that Professor Pittman shared with them.

The group was growing quite rapidly and the seeds were growing as well. Treasure received some help from his mother, who helped him train the other youngsters. The group had grown to over two hundred youngsters, who got their hands dirty with cow dung and mud. They enjoyed it. They played and threw the dung in each other's faces. When they worked, the poverty seemed to disappear.

Their passion grew stronger and the Young Kings and Queens became more tenacious and persevered. Treasure taught his peers how to start their own gardens at home to grow food for their families. His friends were watching, learning and starting food gardens at their own homes.

For weeks, the scholars gathered every day at the African Juniper tree at the riverbank. The tree barely had leaves on it, but it was the only African Juniper tree in Sululta. The youngsters educated each other beneath that tree and they called that place, the Chamber.

Kidane and his friends always gathered and scoffed at them, making fun of what they were doing, but Treasure told them not to pay attention to anything anyone said. The scholars taught each other, taking turns and sharing everything they had learnt with one another. They were passionate and determined.

Not only did they gather to learn but also the youngsters sang and danced. They accepted everyone and discriminated against no one. Everyone was equal, regardless of gender, ethnic group or religion.

After singing a song, Treasure stood up, "Young Kings and Queens, we have done so much in just two months," he said. "I know you guys enjoy being outside and doing all of this… but let's face the truth. We're still dying, the kids are still dying… We need help from the Americans… We cannot do it alone. We need to get the word out there before the famine destroys us. Every day, more than one hundred children die because of malnutrition. We-"

The sound of little voices singing came from a narrow footpath behind them and interrupted Treasure. It was a group of younger graders, eight and nine year olds. The elder scholars were startled and nudged each other.

Lucky was leading them, which was funny because he was almost the same height as they were.

"Ladies and gentlemen," Lucky said. "We have visitors. They said they wanted to be Treasure Hunters, Young Kings and Queens as well." He turned around and shrugged, "Look at their cute faces. I just could not say no to them. We're just going to have to find a way to accommodate everyone." He glanced at Treasure, making an army salute gesture, "So, lead us my fearless leader."

The youngsters took their seats on the dusty floor, folding their tiny bony legs. Their stomachs were growling, their mouths dry, but they had hope and determination.

Treasure cleared his throat where a lump had formed. Such young kids should not have to fight for themselves, he thought. "As you can see brothers and sisters," he croaked. "We have made great examples to those who follow us."

The crowd nodded and smiles beamed on their melancholic faces.

"We have shown true leadership," Treasure said. "We have shown what we can do when we all work together, that we do not have to wait for teachers or anyone to teach us. We can rise up and build the fabric of our own lives." He grew more passionate as he spoke and his voice was shaking. "We will rise up and build Sululta. We will fight for our dreams. We will stand up, bold and fight for our society." He pumped his fist in the air. "It is time to strive towards making a difference, loving and giving more. It is time to change the world. To become engineers, doctors, scientists and world changers. This is our time, this is our moment." Tears began to dripple down his face. "We will never get another opportunity again. We do not get another shot at life. You only get one chance and this is it… you only live once, only once, so I'm going to rise up and fight for a better life."

Veins protruded from his neck, "We are the children and nothing will stop us. You only live once, Young

Kings and Queens. It is time to take control of your lives *right now*! *Don't give up*."

The speech boomed over the Young Kings and Queens, a cacophony of applause and cheering shrouded, echoing through dry tree branches. The Young Kings and Queens were whooping, hollering, clapping, stamping their feet, sprinkled with palpable excitement buzzing through the charged air. There were infectious grins, strangers shaking hands, patting one another on the back and a spontaneous outpouring of emotions. It was a moment in a life time.

Their shouting echoed through the distance to the white clinical tents where Professor Pittman worked. When she heard the shout and all the nurses mumbled beneath their breaths, curious about what was going on, Professor Pittman smiled, shook her head and muttered, "I just knew it."

Kidane and his friends stood at a distance. Their faces were tight and tense. Kidane began to hate Treasure even more. He looked at him through wide, red-rimmed eyes, his mouth slightly open and a shimmer of snot above his cracked lip. "We need to stop this," Kidane hissed. "That boy is getting on my nerves…" he said and beckoned his pals. "C'mon, let's go, I have a plan."

Treasure looked at them walk away as the crowd wailed and cheered, but the look in Kidane's eyes, he didn't like at all.

13

The war broke again. The soldiers killed men in the streets, burning houses and raping women. It was a political riot. All the schools were shut down. A three year old girl was seen weeping over her dead mother, with blood gushing out of her mouth trying to wake her up. Another four year old little girl was seen trying to feed her five month year old sibling with her breast that produced no milk.

Geldof had been procrastinating about his plan for Ethiopia. Nevertheless, one morning when he was sitting on his couch drinking coffee, he was motivated by a BBC news report from Michael Buerk about the famine in Ethiopia that was getting worse.

He leapt off his chair, started calling all the famous pop singers and told them he wanted to write a charity song to raise funds for Ethiopia. Band Aid was the name that they gave their band. It was a super group consisting of mainly the biggest British and Irish musical artists.

On the 3rd December 1984 they released the single in the United Kingdom and aided by considerable publicity, it entered the UK Singles Chart at number one and stayed there for five weeks, becoming the Christmas number one hit of 1984.

'Do they know it's Christmas?' was the name of the song.

***

IN THE AFTERNOON, Lucky, Treasure and Simone sat at the Chamber as the sun shut its eyes behind the mountaintops. They had gathered rocks from the dried river and used it as stones. They were sitting, peering at the bottles filled with sand and cow dung. The bottles were strung next to one another in rows of tens and bundles of fifties. It looked like something kids would use to play with, unlike something that was supposed to feed them.

"How much money did we put together?" Treasure said.

Simone sighed, "A hundred and ninety four birr."

Treasure nodded, "And how many bottles have we filled?"

"Mm," Lucky murmured, reading from a piece of paper. "We have forty batches of fifty… that will make it two thousand."

Treasure brooded, "This is not enough," he said.

Lucky and Simone looked at him, "What do you mean?" Lucky blurted. "Nobody has money Treasure, that's all we could raise… and we did quite well."

"Not as well as we could, if we demanded that everyone who works in our country, give something," he said, frustrated. "And we need the doctors, we need the vitamins. This. This can only cover three schools. And the worst news is… that our community is a warzone. We need to go to Addis Ababa and send that letter… As soon as possible."

Simone's eyes popped open, "HOW SOON?" she blurted out. "Addis Ababa is thirty kilometres from Sululta… That's a six hour walk, Treasure!"

"We don't have much of a choice do we?" Treasure retorted, exasperated. "We will hike along the road…

We will find many tourists there that we can give the letter to."

"Didn't you say we will wait until the seeds grow?" Simone squeaked. "And, I haven't started writing anything."

Treasure shook his head, "No, I don't want to wait anymore. Tomorrow, we're going to Addis Ababa to send that letter," he said and glanced at Lucky, "and tonight, tonight me and you must break into the clinics and steal some more multivitamins and some equipment… I will be teaching every single volunteer everything that Professor Pittman taught me."

Lucky and Simone looked at each other with eyes glittering with fear, "T-Treasure you can't do that? What if we get caught? We'll get in serious trouble-"

"Trouble with who?" Treasure retorted, flailing his hands. "Nobody is doing anything anyways, Simone."

Lucky shook his head, "That is not a good idea. Professor Pittman will get into trouble for that remember. We're not doctors –"

"And little children are not supposed to wander in the fields trying to get to the Save the Child shelter, looking for food," Treasure retorted, seriously with all the muscles of his face taut like he was wearing a mask. "Little children are supposed to be playing, running, singing and being little kids… not here, beneath this dying tree, working on something that will not even provide enough food to sustain us for a week… we need more, we need to do more."

They could see the frustration in Treasure's face. Lucky knew that look; he knew he was going to do it.

He started walking up the hill, "Finish that letter tonight, Simone and we'll meet tomorrow morning right here at four thirty in the morning," he said and glanced at Lucky, "We'll meet at open field where we found that little girl… bring a bag and wear dark clothes." He walked off with his head downcast.

***

TREASURE MADE HIS WAY to Professor Pittman's house and again, without Professor Pittman noticing, he fed Lelo a little bit more multivitamin fluids. Treasure placed the spoon on her lips, "k'esi bilo, k'esi bilo… that's it," Treasure said softly looking around for Professor Pittman. Lelo licked her lips rapidly trying to get more of the sugary taste of the medicine, making sucking noises with her eyes and gaping mouth begging for some more. It was a yellowish liquid in a brown bottle with a sweet citris taste.

Treasure felt no guilt and no shame, all he wanted was for her to recover so he could help the next babies. He hastily clamped the cap onto the medicine bottle, shoved it back into his bag and ripped off his latex gloves. Just before he walked out, on a little table, was a letter from Professor Pittman's organisation, Save the Children, with a red emblem and a sketch of a child spreading her arms, encircled in red.

He peered at the letter,

TO: Professor Cathy Pittman

Ethiopia Missions Teamleader

FROM:

Carolyn Miles

President & CEO

Save the Children, USA

501 Kings Highway East,

Suite 400

Fairfield,

CT 06825

A light bulb beamed on the top of Treasure's head. Maybe he could send the letter to this address and write as if he were Professor Pittman. He looked around, listening for Professor Pittman, picked up the letter, crumbled it and shoved it in his pocket.

He walked out, pulling the door behind him, hung his white scrub on the hook in the passage and then visited with Professor Pittman in the kitchen, having tea and chocolate chip cookies. He took huge bites and chewed rapidly, his stomach growling like a little lion cub.

"How's your gardening project going?" Professor Pittman asked, smiling whilst stirring her tea, with her legs crossed.

Treasure swallowed hard, waiting for the cookies to sink to his stomach before he spoke, he cleared his throat, "We haven't started yet," he croaked. "But everything is fine… it's just that…"

Treasure couldn't tell her that they were planning to start their own training. He brooded for a moment. If he told her he thought they didn't have enough bottles, she would offer some more, but Treasure didn't need more bottles, he needed more medicine now and more doctors.

Professor Pittman ceased stirring and waited for the answer with her head tilted to one side, "It's just what Treasure?"

Treasure exhaled, "It's – it's nothing," he stuttered and stood up getting ready to leave. "I guess, I'm just a bit excited that's all." He chuckled and shrugged, "I mean, I'm getting a lot of support from my mother, she's teaching me a lot about food gardens and Lucky and Simone are also doing a great job, so it's okay." His voice became quite squeaky in the end and Professor Pittman knew that not everything was going okay.

She smiled tight-lipped, but she still thought there was something puzzling about Treasure, "You don't stay nowadays… you're always in a rush to leave… why?" She peered at him with disciplinary intent.

Treasure looked away, gaped and faltered, should he tell her what he wanted to do? If he did, she'd stop him. Should he tell her the truth about feeding Lelo some extra multivitamins? She would be really mad at him, if he did. Should he even tell her that he wanted to send a letter to bring more doctors to Sululta. If he did that, she would suspect he was busy with something bigger than what she told him to do. And of course he couldn't tell her about him planning to break in to her work station that night to steal some multivitamins, that would be stupid.

The silence was a giveaway. Treasure stood at the door cracking his knuckles whilst positioning his bag with his camera on his shoulder.

"You know you can tell me anything right?" Professor Pittman asked.

Treasure nodded, "I know Professor and thank you. But everything is really okay, I promise you." He could feel she was already suspicious about something. This was the second time she asked him about what was bothering him. Perhaps it was just the dream beating beneath his cranium. It made him restless, it made him not desire any more advice from anyone. People seemed too much to be trying to play it safe and he knew if he would listen to anybody, even Professor Pittman, he would never get what he wanted done.

"I just don't want you doing something reckless, alright," she said. "If you're not sure, you can always ask me. It's better to ask than to suffer the consequences of your own mistakes."

Treasure nodded, but it was already too late. His only hope was what she once told him. "Professor," he said in a soft tone. "Do you remember what you said to me…"

Professor Pittman tilted her head to one side, listening.

"You said, if something is important to you, you will always find a way and if it's not, you will always find an excuse… sometimes you will have to break some rules. Whatever it is that you want to do, Just do it, you only live once and let no one tell you what you can and cannot do. You are able and capable."

Professor Pittman smiled and chuckled through her nostrils and nodded, "Yes, yes I remember Treasure."

"This," Treasure said with a serious countenance, eyes wide, "this right here, what I'm doing for Lelo and what I want to do for Sululta is important to me."

Professor Pittman stood with her arms crossed and felt a lump lodge in her throat. The seriousness in his face made her heart prod against her rib cage.

"Thousands of children in Ethiopia are dying," Treasure continued. "And millions around the world still aren't getting what they deserve... in America, your country too... but here, it's worse. We're talking about children in need. Dying, when the world knows how to save them. Vulnerable children in poverty, denied an education, forced to flee violence. Orphaned, abused, abandoned. Children with no reason to smile. No hope for the future... Malnutrition contributes to the deaths of children and a lifetime of poor health... that's what you told me... and I'm going to change that... no child deserves to go to sleep hungry... not even a black child from Africa," Treasure said with sheer heartfelt passion, his eyes welled up with tears. "I cannot wait Professor, I just can't... and if it means getting in trouble, then it's worth it right...?" he stared into her eyes, waiting for her approval.

Professor Pittman gulped and the tears trickled down her cheeks, she nodded, "Yeah, you're right," she croaked with her arms clenched on her chest and her heart heavy.

Treasure paused for a while. "Good bye Professor and thank you for the cookies and tea," Treasure said and walked away with a confident swagger.

She watched him until he was out of sight. Perhaps her greatest decision, was coming back to Sululta.

***

LATER THAT NIGHT, when the moon was at its zenith, the crickets where chirping, the owls hooting and the hyenas laughing, Treasure met with Lucky at the tree where they found the little girl.

Both of them were wearing black and Lucky even had something wrapped over his face.

"What is that on your face?" Treasure whispered.

Lucky peaked around the tree, looking at the UN Military guard circulating the tents with an AK-47 rifle tied over his shoulder, "It's my grandma's pantyhose," he whispered, breathing heavily.

Treasure grimaced, "What's it doing on your face?"

"So they won't see my face," Lucky said.

Treasure shook his head and a hyena laughed in the distance.

Lucky flinched and he felt his heart jump to his throat, "Man, let's hurry up."

"What? It's just a hyena," Treasure said.

"Yeah, they bite too," Lucky retorted. "Look man, it's either we're going to do this now or I'm turning and going home, before I become supper for those hyenas."

Treasure chuckled, looking at how short and tiny Lucky looked in the big black coat he was wearing and the bag dangling down his shoulder, "You mean a snack."

Lucky turned around abruptly, "What?"

Treasure shook his head peaking around the tree, "Never mind," he said. The guard walked to the end of the tents and faced the other way unzipping his trousers to pee. Treasure pulled Lucky by his elbow, "C'mon, quick, let's go."

They tottered on their toes like ballerinas and hopped like rabbits as quietly and as quickly as they could, towards the gate. They darted their big round eyes around then stooped at the corner of the gate. It was quiet and all the nurses and doctors were sleeping in their tents.

"There, it's that one there," Treasure said pointing at the big white tent in the middle encircled by smaller one. "That's where they keep all the multivitamins and the equipment."

"Are you sure?" Lucky said, panting. "

"Yeah, I saw where they put it when I came here looking for Professor Pittman."

"And how do you know there's no one guarding it on the inside?"

Ï don't know," Treasure retorted. "C'mon, let's go," he said and ran. Lucky froze for a while, startled and hissed at Treasure who was now a couple of steps ahead, "Damn, this fool," Lucky grunted and tottered after Treasure looking around to his left and to his right, keeping as low as he could.

They got to a place where there was a slit in between the tents. Treasure peaked inside and there was no one. The boxes were scattered on the long table. Treasure nudged Lucky and signalled towards the boxes, "There, you see."

"Yeah, I see," Lucky said, peaking beneath Treasure. "They're too big to carry."

"We have to open them up," Treasure said. "And take one item in each box."

Lucky squirmed a little, fiddling and reshuffling his feet. His forehead was sweating.

"C'mon, let's go," Treasure said and squeezed himself through the slit in the tent, scanned around and fled to the boxes, with Lucky following him.

Treasure unhooked his bag, stooped on the floor and pulled out a huge knife he had sharpened on a rock, when he got home. He briskly sliced the boxes in the centre of the leaves through the collotype. Lucky followed him inside, but tripped over a box that was placed on the floor, causing a lot of noise.

Treasure flinched and stooped down, "SSSSHHHH," he hissed. "Could you try to be softer? We gonna get caught!"

"Sorry, I tripped, it's dark," Lucky said, writhing and grunting, as he tried to lift himself up.

"Then take that thing off your face."

Lucky pulled off the pantyhose.

"C'mon, hurry up."

They fished in the boxes, pulling out one of each item. There were a lot of things: latex gloves, stethoscopes, hygiene kits, portable cribs, baby wipes, measuring tapes, toys, multivitamins and some dolls.

When Treasure stuffed two dolls in his backpack, Lucky frowned at him, "What are you going to do with that?"'

Treasure glanced at him, "Play house with you," he said and brandished the doll in front of his body, speaking in a little girlish whimpering tone, "hey, my name is Lucky and I'm afraid of the dark. Do you want to play with me-"

"Man, stop playing before someone comes," Lucky hissed.

Treasure laughed, "I'm kidding, I'm going to use them to teach CPR," he said and shoved the toys into his backpack. "I think we have enough stuff now, let's go… There, you take the multivitamins."

"Yeah, I did, let's go…"

When they stuck their heads through the slit, to squeeze themselves out of the tent, Treasure gasped and flinched. The guard stood in front of them, towering like Goliath over David, standing with his arms crossed and his legs spread apart, "Well, well, well," the man drawled. "What do we have here?"

14

The man yanked Treasure's arm and pulled him out of the tent and grabbed Lucky with his left hand. He was so strong that he held both of them as if he was holding dolls in his hands. The strong iron grip of the guard made them wince and grimace, "WHAT ARE YOU DOING HERE?"

"We, we -," Lucky stammered, "we're looking for Prof…"

"We're making a video," Treasure retorted, cutting Lucky short. Treasure fished in his bag, "Look," he said lifting his video camera, "here's the camera. It's a school project, we're making a video…"

The man scanned their eyes, "You're lying to me," he hissed, his eyes resembling vicious viper slits. "You're stealing the children's medicine, I'm arresting you, c'mon…" He pulled them by their arms, they stumbled, whimpered and begged the guard to let them go. "I won't let you go, you're stealing."

Lucky glanced at Treasure who signalled with his head, telling him to get ready to run. Lucky nodded.

While the guard was murmuring and growling, Treasure sunk his teeth into the guards arm, biting him as hard as he could, "C'MON, RUN," he shouted and leapt passed the guard.

Lucky escaped beneath the guard's legs and ran, with big eyes, weighed down by the heavy bag. The guard shouted at them, "Come here, you little infants," trying to catch up with them, but the boys' adrenalin levels was so high that they ran faster than they ever ran before, panting. When the guard saw that they had disappeared into the night, he stopped chasing them, stood at the gate and clicked his tongue, "If you come here again, I'll shoot you, bloody infants," he shouted and walked back.

Treasure and Lucky just continued running, panting and out of breath, thinking that the guard was still behind them. They finally stopped when they reached the front of Lucky's gate, "That was close," Treasure said, winded.

Lucky nodded, breathing heavily, “I’m not going back there again, we have to find another way.”

“You almost told him about Professor Pittman,” Treasure said.

“What was I supposed to do?” Luck retorted, shrugging and exposing his palms. “He was going to arrest us.”

“Yes, but you shouldn’t have brought up Professor Pittman’s name-“

“I didn’t-“

“But you almost did!”

Lucky shook his head, “Man, I don’t have time for this, you should be thankful I went there with you… you want this too much,” Lucky said walking away inside his gate, exasperated. “You’re gonna mess it up, Treasure, I’m part of this too remember and you need to learn how to listen to me too,” Lucky said and walked inside his house.

Treasure stood there humbled. He could see in Lucky’s face how serious he was and he couldn’t afford to lose him; he needed him just as much as he needed to make his dream a reality. Maybe Lucky was right, he thought. He almost got them in trouble. However, what else could he do? There was no other way. He made his way home in the dark and climbed through the window. He perched on his bed, thinking of what almost happened. His heart was still pounding.

The same thoughts rose to defend his actions. "You have to save those kids. It's my purpose. They should just live a life worth living. Breaking rules is not a problem." Nevertheless, it bothered him and he went to sleep, still trembling about what could have happened.

***

THE NEXT DAY TREASURE apologised to Lucky. He knew he'd done something pretty awful when he had to work so hard to justify it, "I guess you're right," Treasure said. "Maybe I am obsessed."

"There's nothing wrong with obsession," Lucky said. "It's just that… it's just that sometimes I tend to think you're making this too much about you and what you want. Remember why Professor Pittman gave you that story. It's about unity and teamwork. We need to come to mutual decisions before we can take the next step, that's the only way we can make this work. I want to be part of the process and not feel forced, because technically, I don't need to be here. But I believe in your dream… and I believe in you… but if you continue like this… I'm gone."

Treasure nodded and felt the words pierce his heart. The guilt sat not in his chest but inside his head. He apologised wholeheartedly and they made their way towards the school. They couldn't use the tree they gathered at to train the other kids, so they broke inside the school at night and used the Biology classroom.

Lucky invited all the senior students in his school who could read, write and who wanted to make a difference. That was his gift and talent, to bring people together.

"I know it's late and most of you are tired," Treasure said. "But there's nothing we can do… if we want to have a great future for the children of this community, we need to work hard on that… we will work hard every day and every night towards our illustrious dream of abundant living… we will not accept middle class, sickness and poverty as a birth right. We will crave success, wealth and good health for our people. We need to make the choice to choose optimal health and challenge the limits of our physical abilities in every way and when the Americans come, WE WILL BE READY…"

The scholars felt the adrenalin stream through their bodies. They felt what Treasure was saying and it gave them goose pimples.

Treasure continued to speak relentlessly, "We all have a gift inside of us," he said. "A gift that will benefit others, not just ourselves. This is a Treasure to the world. We are Treasure Hunters, so we will look for that gift inside of us and we will use it to change the world… We need to have courage and go against the grain. The key to living a more fulfilling life is to find our gifts and then live using them to change the world. Only you know what your gift is in life, only you know what dream you have… my dream, my dream is to save lives and change lives. Change is within reach – if we have courage, determination, imagination and effective organisation. Our mission here is one of hope, of deeply passionate and committed people, determined to make the world a better place for all our children. And if you don't want this… then you probably don't belong here… Your life is a message to the world, make sure your message is inspiring, your life is filled with love, compassion and passion. Your life is a gift… A gift you will not have for long. A gift that has no guarantees. You need to make the most out of your life and your gift. Go after your purpose and destiny, go after your dreams, fight for what you want, take risks if you have to, WE CANNOT fail if we work together and use our gifts, our gifts will make a way for us… You only live once, but if you do it right, once is enough, my friends…"

***

TREASURE GATHERED all the adolescent scholars every night in the same room, same time for six weeks and taught them all that Professor Pittman had taught him. He divided them into groups of five. There were thirty three volunteers in total.

Through the door-to-door approach, they sought to effect health and social behavioural changes through their interactions with household members and increasing awareness around particular health issues. The elders were in awe of the knowledge that the Young Kings and Queens had. Treasure created a team of sport volunteers who mobilised the youth, towards being involved in sports as part of behavioural change. They were the Youth as Agents of Behavioural change and everything was going well.

They also helped with daily activities such as dressing, bathing, toileting and arranging childcare. Treasure tasked them with and explained the importance of providing support and encouragement for the children as well as themselves. "Communication is key in the relationship between a caregiver and a patient," Treasure told them. "It is important to both openly share feelings and remain empathetic to the situation. Be available to listen. Be sure people we interact with, know that we are available should they need something. Be available for those who want to discuss a topic privately or more in depth after an educational workshop or session. Always listen in a non-judgmental way. We are here to save lives and change lives, not to seek to make a name for ourselves… We're a dynamite team of Young Kings and Queens who're ready to kick some ass," he continued and the youngsters laughed and giggled.

Their primary goal was to improve the well-being of vulnerable children and youth and increase their likelihood of growing up to be healthy, educated and socially well-adjusted adults, by providing them with a comprehensive package of services, promoting HIV status knowledge, strengthening capacity of caregivers and families to address their needs. Their objectives included: mitigated the impact of HIV to orphaned, vulnerable children and youth, under 18 years of age; strengthening the capacity of the caregivers and families to address key issues facing children, malnutrition, including sexual risk behavior and prevention of neglect, violence and exploitation.

It was a wonderful thing to experience, but the only problem was - that the word of their work was spreading fast.

"No one knows when the next earthquake, flood or tsunami will strike," Treasure said, instructing. "But we do know that children are severely affected by everything that happens, especially natural disasters. They also suffer greatly during conflict, drought and disease outbreaks, like now. This is our natural disaster response and emergency relief programme to help protect vulnerable little boys and girls during disasters and their aftermath. So you, everyone in here is a Young King and Queen."

One girl lifted up her hand, "But it never rains here and there are no earthquakes?"

Treasure brooded for a while, "I know, but it's always better to stay prepared. And besides, what I've taught you, you can use now… children are already dying. So you can already begin helping them… but on one condition… all of you must work in pairs and all of you must do exactly what I taught you or don't do it at all… we can't help a dead baby."

"We are on the ground now," Treasure said. "And we will be rebuilding the fabric of our own communities… whilst we wait for the Americans," Treasure added. "We are going to be providing lifesaving support to children and families in response to this devastating food crisis. Our priority is to reach children under age five, who are less able to withstand malnutrition and are more susceptible to disease.

"We will divide ourselves into teams, some will be screening children for malnutrition, some will be running feeding programmes and only I will treat malnourished children. Once our programme is recognised, we will refer those who are very ill to health centres. When it rains, we will also provide clean water, address sanitation and hygiene to prevent diseases from spreading and provide support to families who've lost everything. We will also provide health education and care to children in need, through our school health programmes to help children stay healthy, well nourished and in school. Each one, teach one. I'm talking from experience, I've taught my mother how to read… and so can you… Every child in Africa deserves to know how to read a good story… and you are going to teach them."

Some of the students' eyes widened, "How are we going to do all of that?" one boy asked. "This is all we have."

There were some murmurs of agreement while some said that the food gardens wouldn't be enough, nor would the medicine.

Treasure brooded for a while and lifted his hand to silence the hubbub, "I don't know," he finally said when silence reigned. "But I believe the Americans are coming-"

"And what if they don't," one girl retorted.

"Then we will just continue doing what we're doing, until something happens," Treasure said. "But we won't sit and wait… Good things come to those who work and wait in faith. We just have to have faith, that's all we need. If we have hope, we can persevere till the end… We are Young Kings and Queens… and our country is full of Treasure. We will call our programme

Treasure Hunting. Not because of my name, but because of the Treasure you have inside, which are gifts and talents, because of the Treasure in our societies… We will rise up and build."

Treasure had laid out a plan of what their 'movement' was all about, so that everyone who joined could understand their mission.

THE TREASURE HUNT

Treasuring Hunting is an intention to build solidarity and agency (Capacity Building). Building on a community's treasures rather than focusing on its needs for future development is the basic treasure hunting approach. By focusing on successes and small triumphs instead of looking at what is missing or negative about a place, a positive community outlook and vision for the future can be fostered. Communities are built from the treasures and gifts of the community and not on needs or deficiencies.

Terms meanings:

- Cave Digging - Capacity building

- Island - Community
- Treasure Map - meaning assessment of resources and assets within the community (cave).
- Looking for footprints – Collecting data.

The Treasure hunting approach is based on the principle of identifying and mobilising individual and community 'assets or resources', rather than focusing on problems and needs (i.e. 'deficits').

Treasure Hunting is a set of values and principles which:

- Identify and makes visible the health-enhancing treasure in a community
- Sees citizens and their Islands (communities) as the co-producers of health and well-being, rather than the recipients of services
- Promote Island (community) networks, relationships and friendships that can

provide caring, mutual help and empowerment

- Identify what has the potential to improve health and well-being
- Support individuals' health and well-being through self-esteem, coping strategies, resilience skills, relationships, friendships, knowledge and personal resources
- Empower communities to control their futures and create tangible resources such as services, funds and buildings.

What are Treasures?

A health asset is: "any factor or resource which enhances the ability of individuals, communities and populations to maintain and sustain health and well-being. These assets can operate at the level of the individual, family or community as protective and promoting factors to buffer against life's stresses."

Other assets include the following:

- the practical skills, capacity and knowledge of local residents
- the passions and interests of local residents that give them energy for change
- the networks and connections – known as 'social capital' – in a community, including friendships and neighbourliness
- the effectiveness of local community and voluntary associations
- the resources of public, private and third sector organisations that are available to support a community
- the physical and economic resources of a place that enhance well-being.

Using a treasure hunt approach enables communities to build on the treasure they already have to gain what they need and make improvements to their community, thereby improve individual and community level health and well-being.

Like the Young King and Queen, self-improvement is not what it's all about, although it plays a part of it, it is not the core of improvement. To bring change in any community, school, church, institution or organisation is a collective voluntary sweat equity which starts from a shift in your mind set about your connectedness. If the Young King and Queen had continued to think of themselves individually, they would have died on the Island. When they sought to build social capital and discover what treasures they had, instead of what they lacked, they ended up reaching their goals.

They took these three steps;

1. They focused on their treasure. Even though there was conflict at first, they resolved it.

2. They valued each other's associations and there was no hierarchy of authority. They were equally valued and they all began to show that they needed each other.

3. They realised that they had to rise up, build and take action to change the fabric of their own lives.

They also followed these three linear sequences:

Capacity Building: they discovered their capacity and mobilised what they had.

Social Capital: Once they discovered what treasure they had, both externally in terms of the natural resources, they also realised they needed each other. This enabled them to develop the ability to act.

Community Development Outcome: After working together they were able to meet their needs.

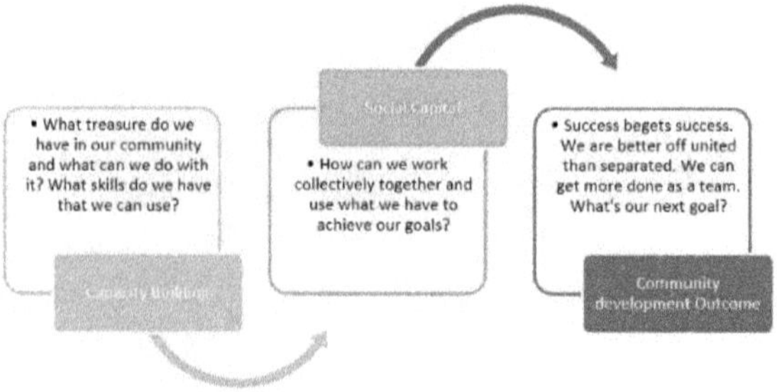
• What treasure do we have in our community and what can we do with it? What skills do we have that we can use?
• How can we work collectively together and use what we have to achieve our goals?
• Success begets success. We are better off united than separated. We can get more done as a team. What's our next goal?
Community development Outcome

THE PROCESS

This next section introduces a general outline of the treasure hunt approach and describes its major steps.

STEP 1: CONNECT GROUP ORGANISING

Connect Group Organising focuses on getting people within your community, school, church, organisation, neighbourhood or company together for a common goal. Simply put, connect Group Organising can be thought of as a way to bring together small groups of people to accomplish a particular task.

Bringing together people within your community, school, university, church or school, involves direct action ranging from writing letters of invitation to organising a community dialogue to discuss how you can use the community treasure to solve community disintegration. The essential test is to change from solitary to solidarity within your community and into connectedness and caring for the whole, love one another. You begin by shifting your attention from the trash in the community to the treasure in the community.

Often Connect Group Organising uses a problem based approach rather than a treasure based approach. This is where you organise people to "solve" a problem that exists in your community, school, university or church.

There are two methodologies to bring people together:

1. Problem based method (PBM): Social action campaigns that aim to change decisions, societal structures and cultural beliefs e.g. campaigning to raise awareness about the killing of people living with Albinism or campaigning to raise awareness about black lives matter.

2. Goal Based Method (GBM): This is a way to organise people to achieve a variety of goals that have not yet been achieved e.g. to start a food garden project in schools.

STEP 2: VISIONING

The term vision is mostly used by organisations and companies. Treasure Hunting involves establishing a vision that will focus on specific areas, such as teenage drug abuse, unprotected sex, environmental, economic and behavioural challenges.

It is also useful to create multiple topical visions that can be more detailed and focused rather than creating broad visions, which are too vague and unfocused to bring meaning to the necessary actions. The basic idea is to gather a wide range of individuals, associations and groups within your community or school to arrive at a written vision statement that was collectively agreed upon. This is the vision for the future and to help prepare an action plan to move the Connect Group towards the vision.

There are three imperative components of a vision exercise. (1) Inviting a variety of different peers without discrimination based on religion, gender, ethnic group, race, skin colour, beliefs, culture or preferences of social group. This is to allow opinions and perspectives to be shared and brainstormed without any judgement.

(2) Is preparing a process that is meaningful, effective, productive and efficient. The process must be meaningful so that volunteers can be motivated by meaningful and achievable results. The process must be effective because it seeks to fulfil a common problem that would benefit the whole group and others indirectly. The process must be efficient because people do not want to waste their time and energy for something they will not be rewarded for. And finally, the process must be productive because results are the most important aspect of a project. (3) The final one, is participation from other peers to help accomplish the vision. Teamship is a very important aspect. Participation helps in brainstorming, assessing the Strengths, Weaknesses, Opportunities and Threats and helps to put together a plan to accomplish the connect group's purpose.

STEP 3: PLANNING

During the planning stage there are three most important tasks in preparing an action plan: (1) Collecting footprints and analysing, (2) Treasure map, and (3) a Cave survey.

(1) Collecting footprints and analysing involves trying to understand the current circumstances, the changes that are occurring inside your cave over time and the implications of the data.

(2) Treasure map is the process of acquainting yourself and learning about the treasures that are available in your community.

The process involves assessing the capacity of:

- Individuals including other youth, seniors, people with disabilities, local artists and others.
- Local associations and organisations including local businesses, charity groups, ethnic associations, political organisations,

service clubs, sport leagues, religious institutions and many others.

- Local institutions for community uplifting including parks, libraries, schools, community colleges, police hospitals and any other institutions.

Treasure mapping is an ongoing process. The main idea of the process is to recognise the local treasure, knowledge and resources within the community.

(3) A Cave survey is useful in identifying problems at the beginning stages of the planning process and to develop ideas and write up policies as the community begins to brainstorm about its goals and action plans.

A Cave survey will allow the Connect Group to:

- Gather information about attitudes and opinions regarding defined issues, problems and opportunities faced by youth.

- Determine the youth priority problems that need immediate actions in order of importance.
- Give the youth a voice in policy making,
- Identify public support for youth initiatives,
- Evaluate current programmes and policies,

Cave surveys can communicate important information about peer attitudes and opinions. This methodology only focuses on input and not shared decision making. If this process is carried out well, it will allow for a much broader range of peers to participate than any other participation technique that requires face-to-face interaction.

STEP 4: PARTICIPATION

The most important part of digging our caves is to determine how we will get from point A to point B. Often, young people leave major goals and decisions to elders, the government or to authority. This could be for many reasons, fear of authority and upbringing. However, young people need to participate and get actively involved in determining the future course of digging the cave. If they do not, others will determine their future for them. Participation is crucial to the cave digging process.

Getting people to participate is perhaps the most difficult part of the cave digging process. Effective participation needs to be both functional for the specific goal and meaningful to the other peers.

Participation is functional when it helps to create better decisions and establish better plans or programme proposals that can help the Connect Group to move forward. It is also meaningful when it helps to create opportunities for the public to help exercise influence over decisions and feel a sense of ownership towards the product.

STEP 5: IMPLEMENTATION AND EVALUATION

Taking action in the cave digging process is where change occurs. This is the stage where you just do it. This is the point where the rubber meets the road. It is the phase where individuals, groups and organisations are active rather than passive participants in helping dig their caves. Up until this stage, your peers and yourself have made a concerted effort to understand and to discover the treasures, peer attitudes and opinions and have arrived at a shared understanding of the future and have agreed upon the initial actions in the future.

Action plans identify specific projects, deadlines, responsible parties, funding mechanisms and other tasks that will accomplish specific goals. Action plans are a set of activities that move the group toward its future vision and other goals.

You will have to monitor and evaluate the cave digging process. Monitoring is the act of assessing the cave digging process as it is taking place. It is almost like taking the pulse of a patient. It allows for changes to be made in the process rather than allowing things to get worse and beyond the control of the steering committee and the project team.

Evaluation, in contrast, usually occurs when the project is completed or has gone through a certain period of time. Evaluation measures two types of accomplishments: Outputs- the direct and short-term results of a project plan such as the number of peers trained in food gardening, the number of peers fed through the food garden project.

Then outcomes are the long-term results of the project. These are much more difficult to measure. An outcome may be something like, decreased levels of poverty or increased numbers in income.

To be successful, young people need to develop skills such as: thinking, taking responsibility and making the most of their potential.

TREASURE HUNTING PLAN

OUR SLOGAN

"You Only Live Once"

OUR COMMUNITY DEVELOPMENT PROCESS:

- Establish an organising group
- Create a vision and mission statement

- Identify community stakeholders
- Collect and analyse information
- Develop an effective communication process
- Expand the organisation
- Create a comprehensive strategic plan
- Identify the local leadership and establish a plan management team to liaise and lobby the local leadership
- Implement plan
- Review and evaluate the planning outcomes
- Celebrate the success
- Create new goals and objectives.

OUR GOAL

- Reach out to our peers across Ethiopia.

- Seek partnerships with private, public organisations. Churches and civil societies.

OUR MISSION:

- Care for and love one another.
- Change the world and touch lives.
- Find the treasure in our communities and in our peers.

OUR VISION:

"We treasure...

- A clean and green natural environment- Free from litter. Clean water. Saving water...
- A supportive community- People are friendly. We want an easy lifestyle where young people can be safe and supported by elders and where young people respect everyone and are compassionate towards elders and the disabled.
- A zero HIV and AIDS infection rate amongst teenagers.

- A young society with Zero unwanted teenage pregnancies.
- A non-racial, non-sexist and democratic society.
- No bullying and violence in schools.
- No drugs and alcohol.
- No sex before marriage.

<u>OUR LIFE MOTIVATION</u>

- We are motivated by the gift of life and we want to make the best out of it.

<u>OUR PLEDGE</u>

- We agree to connect every week
- We are not aligned to any political principles and we will stay committed to find treasure.
- We will respect each other by showing up to The Chamber Group consistently and starting/ending on time.

- We will all share responsibility and pull our own weight.
- We will do our best to notice each other's growth and care when tough things happen – both during and outside group time.
- We will treat everyone with respect and dignity.
- We will create a high-performance, high-trust culture of honesty and remain committed to excellence.
- We will work to develop a good understanding of our work situation and the career aspirations of our peers.
- We will endeavour to help each other learn, grow and realise our career ambitions.
- We will work to continuously upgrade the environment and keep it safe, green and clean.

- We will share our assessment of our current circumstances and future potential with our peers, solicit input, support and responsibly empower each to rise and build.
- We will work diligently to keep our commitments. We will act with integrity. We will endeavour to do everything we say we are going to do.
- If we fall short of a commitment, we will openly and honestly acknowledge our shortcoming and conscientiously work to remedy the situation.

DAILY CODE OF CONDUCT

- ATTITUDE:

Choose and display the right attitude daily.

- HEALTH

Know and follow healthy daily guidelines

- FAMILY

Communicate with and care for family daily

- THINKING

Practice and develop good thinking daily

- COMMITMENT

Make and keep proper commitments daily

- FAITH

Deepen and live out your faith daily

- RELATIONSHIPS

Initiate and invest in solid relationships daily

- GENEROSITY

Plan for and model generosity daily

- GROWTH

Seek and experience improvements daily.

- LOVE AND COMPASSION

  Love and care for everyone regardless of their religion, gender or background.

<u>OUR VALUES</u>

- Honesty
- Loyalty
- Fairness
- Courage
- Caring
- Respect
- Tolerance
- Duty
- Lifelong learning

OUR LEADERSHIP QUOTE

"I do not choose to be a common man,

It is my right to be uncommon ... if I can,

I seek opportunity ... not security."

"I do not wish to be a kept citizen.

Humbled and dulled by having the

State look after me.

"I want to take the calculated risk;
To dream and to build.
To fail and to succeed.

"I refuse to barter incentive for a dole;
I prefer the challenges of life
To the guaranteed existence;
The thrill of fulfillment
To the stale calm of Utopia.

"I will not trade freedom for beneficence
Nor my dignity for a handout
I will never cower before any master
Nor bend to any threat.

"It is my heritage to stand erect.

Proud and unafraid;

To think and act for myself,

Enjoy the benefit of my creations

And to face the world boldly and say:

This, with God's help, I have done.

_By Dean Alfange

Treasure made sure that everyone who joined the group, knew what they were all about. Their group was growing fast, from thirty-three to one hundred and fifty scholars. The room was becoming too small to house them all and they called their room, The Chamber.

The Chamber included bringing everyone who was interested together, electing the Chairperson (everyone of course voted for Treasure), Deputy Chairperson (in which everyone of course voted for Lucky) and appointing the Secretary (everyone voted for Simone). Everything was going as they had planned. Lucky, Simone and Treasure called themselves The Workers and everybody else they called The Hunters.

The Workers were responsible for lobbying and intervening with authorities on a higher level. The Hunters were responsible for caregiving and represented their movement.

They had a horizontal structure where no one had more authority than the other did. Everyone was equal.

A group of new volunteers came to Lucky and asked him what the programme was about. These youngsters saw the fun that they were having and the impact they had on the community.

"Our mission is about changing minds by touching hearts," Lucky said. "It is rooted in a participant-centred, experiential learning approach and relies on a non-cognitive methodology, meaning that feelings, experience, or the physical body, rather than intellectual analysis are the entry points for learning. Participants are introduced to thematic issues or foster personal skills through games, role-plays, simulation and visualisation exercises, storytelling, artistic platforms and internal arts."

The new youngsters were beaming with interest. Lucky had a unique way of presenting the programme. He was a natural and Treasure himself could not meet his standards. He continued, "We also use peer education to move learners out of their comfort zones," Lucky said, "but at the same time, creating a safe and respectful environment where they are not told what to think or do but where solutions are explored together. Learning comes from within an exchange with peers, at a level of equality and trust, so that individuals develop their own position and commitment through critical reflection," he pointed at the Treasure Hunt plan they had stuck against the wall. "So if you guys want to be a part of us, you'll have to read that first, say the pact… and you'll be a Treasure Hunter."

The youngsters assented and made their way to the board and read everything aloud and Lucky made them solemnly agree to the pact and they were in. He took them to meet the others and the classroom was a cacophony of laughter, playing and talking. Everything they did had a domino effect that impacted and frequently improved their peers and relationships as well and more significantly, the dynamics of their family unit as a whole.

Treasure was busy teaching an activity and experiment for social inclusion. He specifically did this because most of the volunteers were a bit scared of

Lucky because of his pale skin. They didn't understand albinism. They thought he was 'different' from them.

Treasure walked up and down between the scholars with his hands clenched behind his back, teaching the scholars as if he was a real university Professor. He had spent a long time reading and studying.

"All communities," he said, "have groups of people – often hidden – who are unable to enjoy the general benefits that are accessible to 'mainstream' society (i.e., the majority). Such disadvantaged groups can include: women and girls; older people; those living with HIV/AIDS or disabilities; people of a particular sexual orientation; people with albinism…" when he said this everyone looked at Lucky.

Lucky chuckled and blurted out, "That's me!"

The scholars laughed and giggled and so did Treasure and Simone. "Yes, Lucky our Deputy Chair," Treasure added and continued. "Disadvantaged groups are very vulnerable to discrimination, exclusion and violence."

"What makes us a part of our society," he said, "is a feeling of belonging, the things we have in common with other people in our society, the ability to actively participate in the society, whatever the reason, when someone is part of a society, there is a connection between them and that society. In social exclusion, that connection is broken. Something happens that means that a person or even a small group is no longer an active part of 'mainstream' society; they live on the fringe of society.

"Exclusion can be voluntary," Treasure said. "If someone decides that they do not want to be a part of or participate in 'mainstream' society. However, most excluded persons or groups are not given the choice to be a part of society; in fact, they are often actively kept out by those who are part of 'mainstream' society or by the system itself (social exclusion). For instance, imagine a person who is not allowed to have access to education or housing or health services and who is not allowed to vote or make decisions. That person is not able to take part in the life of the society; they are excluded. This is the case with children living with disabilities who cannot have access to 'mainstream' education apart from special schools for the disabled. It is also the case with illegal migrants, i.e., those without valid permits who stay in a country, risk being deported if they try to participate in the life of the society by sending their children to school or to a hospital, for instance.

"Exclusion may come about because a person or a group of people is considered 'different' from the majority of the society and discriminated against on that basis," he said. "Exclusion and discrimination are linked and have underlying root causes, such as ignorance, intolerance, fear of the 'unknown' or 'otherness'. Exclusion can then be seen as a further expression of discrimination. Migrants, for instance, can often face exclusion in society because of the differences of their language, culture or religion – on the basis of which they are treated differently: in other words, discriminated against.

Treasure clapped his hands, "So, we're going to do something fun," he said. "An experiment. To experience how people living with disabilities may be included or excluded from society as a result of stereotypes, prejudices and consequent stigmatisation and discrimination."

Before starting, Treasure let participants know that there were various stages in the activity and that they would be guided through them. He also ensured that they clearly understood the theme given to their group.

He told them to be sensitive to the profiles of their participants and aware that some may feel uncomfortable about physical closeness to others. Therefore, they had to keep an eye on participants' physical proximity to one another and ensure they had a room or open space, either inside or outside, that was large enough for them to be able to move around and create their respective group sculptures, without disturbing each other.

In addition, he told them to make sure that participants felt at ease with each other and considered forming groups of the same sex if that was more appropriate. Then he stressed that physical contact with each other is not necessary and may not be welcomed by other participants during the human sculptures exercises.

Finally, he told them to pay particular attention to the tension that the activity could cause and, therefore, to the division and/or the emotional, psychological or physical violence that it may generate among or between participants. He took them through a six-step activity to teach them about social inclusion.

He divided the participants into at least two different groups and a few members of each group were allocated particular disabilities for use in a role-play. Each group first had to create a human sculpture representing a 'negative' theme, in which the 'disabled' members of the group would feel excluded. Each group then had to create another human sculpture representing a 'positive' theme - this time; the 'disabled' members of the group would feel welcomed and accepted. Finally, participants compared the two processes and reflected on the mind-sets, attitudes and behaviours that promoted non-discrimination and inclusion of people living with disabilities in society.

Things were fun and things were awesome, they laughed and sang, they were united with love and compassion and they had forgotten about all their poverty and shortcomings. However, the problem remained, that the word was spreading too fast and if the word got to Professor Pittman, she would know that

Treasure and Lucky were the ones who broke into the clinics.

15

Professor Pittman had setup tents at her plot of land. This is where she taught the older scholars. No child will live without a decent education.

Whilst Professor Pittman was teaching Biology in the late afternoon, Mr Belay, the School Headmaster walked in, followed by the guard from where Treasure and Lucky stole the medical supplies. Lucky and Treasure sank in their seats and dropped their chins into their chests, not daring to look up.

"Mr Belay," Professor Pittman greeted.

"Professor Pittman," Mr Belay said. "May I have a word with your class please?"

Professor Pittman agreed and Mr Belay greeted the scholars. "A couple of weeks ago," Mr Belay started, "someone broke into the Save the Children clinic and stole a lot of medical supplies and attire. It is believed that it was one of our students." Mr Belay glanced at the guard and pointed at him, "Mr Abera is the guard who was on duty that day and he is here to try and identify the people who were responsible," he glanced at Mr Abera, "you may proceed."

Lucky and Treasure's hearts were stampeding like a herd of buffalo. The closer the guard came to Treasure, the faster his heartbeat rocketed.

Mr Abera strutted through the rows, scanning everyone in their eyes. At this time, Lucky had thrown his white hat over his eyes. The class was ghost quiet and all eyes of the scholars were wide, their breathing shallow and all you could hear was the sound of Mr Abera's boots on the floor.

Kidane emitted a pompous snigger, with a lopsided smirk and raised his hand, "Mr Belay," he said, "…I know who it was…"

Treasure and Lucky flinched, sinking a little lower. Kidane was about to snitch on them, but how did he know?

Kidane stretched his arm and pointed at Lucky, "It was him… the Shanqella boy."

The guard turned his gaze and his eyes darted, "Yes, this is the boy," Mr Abera said, his face getting tighter and vicious as though the felony had just been committed. “I remember him, he was there. Come here.” He leapt towards Lucky and yanked his hat from his head.

Lucky relented stiffening his body as the guard pulled him out of his chair. Lucky didn’t deny that it was him, nor did he object that it wasn’t; he didn’t utter a word.

Of course the guard knew it was him, Lucky was the only one in his class with the pale skin.

The class murmured in awe, startled. You could have expected something like that from Kidane, but Lucky? Lucky would have never done something like that.

Treasure tried to say something, but Lucky shook his head slightly telling him to keep quiet.

“Where’s your friend,” Mr Abera barked, rattling Lucky by his arm. “TALK, where’s your friend?”

“He-He’s not here,” Lucky whimpered, stammering.

“You’re LYING,” Mr Abera shouted. “You’re hiding him.”

"I'm not, he's not from this school."

Professor Pittman peered at Treasure and Treasure dropped his gaze out of guilt and shame. Lucky only had one friend and she knew it was Treasure.

The guard pulled Lucky by his arm to the van and told him that they would arrest him unless he revealed his friend. Everyone was startled, including Mr Belay. He thought it was so unlike Lucky to do something like that.

Mr Belay walked out to the van and scolded Lucky expressing how disappointed he was.

"I'm sorry, Mr Belay," Lucky murmured dropping his head to his feet.

Mr Belay was a goodhearted man of compassion and he felt sorry for him. "Why did you do it?" Mr Belay commanded.

Lucky brooded downcast and looked up again, "I can't tell you right now sir, but soon, you'll know it was for the good of all of us."

Mr Belay stared at him as the guard shut the door of the van. The scholars ran out of the class to look at what happened to Lucky. Treasure stared at Lucky as the van drove away. He felt a lump lodge in his throat and Lucky pumped his fist at Treasure.

Treasure felt his heart jolt. He knew it was time. Simone stood beside him and he felt her put her hand on his. Professor Pittman saw it and she knew the three youngsters were up to something.

Treasure had made up his mind that he was going to Addis Ababa to send the letter to the Americans.

***

TREASURE DIDN'T go to Professor Pittman's house that afternoon and sat beneath the African Juniper Tree. His heart was heavy with remorse and guilt. Everyone was upset and downcast.

"I apologise for embarrassing you guys," he said, his voice trembling. "I haven't been an example and it's my fault that Lucky was arrested, he had warned me about this… but I swear to you… I will get him back… for the time being…" he scanned The Hunters in their eyes and his pupils glittered, filled with tears. "I will have to stop the programme, we will no longer be meeting… There is no Chamber and we're not Treasure Hunters… we're just boys and girls in poverty," he wept. "I'm sorry," he said and ran away.

The Hunters froze and murmured, dropping their heads dolefully and slumping their bodies.

Simone ran after him shouting his name.

Treasure stopped, “WHAT,” he snapped.

“What are you doing?” she said, squeaking.

“What do you think I’m doing,” he growled. “It’s over, this whole thing is just stupid, I just got my best friend in trouble. Lucky is arrested because of me, I did it.”

“Lucky would have wanted you to continue, Treasure,” Simone said, “not give up like this-“

“Who’s gonna bail him out of jail Simone, uh, who?”

Simone exhaled, tears welled up in her eyes, “You said we are a team right. If we get this to work, they will see the importance of the programme, then-“

“Then what Simone?” Treasure shouted. “Arrest more of us…It’s over,” He walked away but Simone continued behind him.

“I’m not quitting Treasure,” she said. “Tomorrow… tomorrow let’s take that letter to Addis

Ababa… that's the least we could do… do it for Lucky… We didn't come this far to quit."

Treasure stopped walking. She was right. He stood downcast, brooding. There was a surge of silence, "FINE," he blurted out. "Meet me here at five o'clock in the morning." He walked away with brisk and long strides.

Simone stood and watched him, pained. She turned around and saw The Hunters walking away slowly. Their faces and heads sagged and their hearts were strewn to pieces like broken glasses.

***

WHEN TREASURE got closer to his house, he heard his mother wailing from the depths of her throat. He ran and bashed the door open, shouting his name. She wasn't in the dining room, she wasn't in the kitchen, she wasn't in her room, she was in Treasure's room.

The room was messed up and turned upside down. Mrs Wedu lay on the ground whimpering, her nose full of blood.

Blazing with rage and fury Treasure stormed towards his father and tackled him to the floor. He punched him and punched him, until he couldn't punch anymore. He felt his knuckles crack on his father's skull and he felt a tooth break loose. His mother leapt up, screaming at Treasure to stop, "You're gonna kill him, you're gonna kill him!" she shouted, pulling Treasure off him.

Mr Wedu stumbled, hoisting himself up from the floor and slipped on the blood and beer that had spilt on the floor. His nose was bleeding, his eyes were owlish, depicting shock. He bumped from wall to wall, when he got up and fled out of the door, running as fast as he could, glancing back abruptly to see if Treasure was running behind him. It was as though he was running away from a monster.

Treasure leapt off the floor and checked his video camera. He rifled in his bag. Sjoe, he found it untouched!

"Where did you get that?" his mother asked, wide-eyed. She had never seen it.

Treasure ignored her and looked around, he opened his savings tin, where he had saved the money for posting... His father had stolen the money.

He grunted and shouted aloud.

"What's wrong?" his mother asked, wide-eyed. "And where did you get that?"

Treasure threw his hands on his head, gritting his teeth, grunting about how he was gonna kill his father; saliva dripped out of the corners of his mouth. His jaw went into a spasm.

"TREASURE," his mother shouted, "I'm talking to you, where did you get that?"

"FROM PROFESSOR PITTMAN," he snapped, exasperated. "She gave it to me, when it was my birthday," he grunted again. "I use it to make videos, so we can send it to the Americans. And that bastard stole the money we were going to use to send the video."

Mrs Wedu brooded, her heart severely distressed. Treasure couldn't keep his feet still, he wept and groaned, "I swear I'm gonna kill that man," repeatedly.

Mrs Wedu had never seen so much anger coming from her son. The anger he had bottled in for years was now oozing out of him. His knuckles had turned pale and veins popped out of his forehead. If Mr Wedu was in front of him, he would snap his neck into pieces.

“Son,” his mother finally said in soft tone when Treasure began to calm down, perched on his bed, with his head dropped between his legs. “Son,” his mother said again and he looked up, “I need to tell you something.”

Treasure darted a sideways glance at her, breathing heavily.

Mrs Wedu contemplated deeply for a moment. Should she tell him the truth? That the father he knew was not his Father? She had to do it, “That man, is not your father…” she croaked, her voice trembling.

Treasure looked up at her, “What?”

She wept and tears dripped down her face, she shook her head, “That is not your father… We are not your parents.”

Treasure’s eyes widened and he leapt up, “What are you saying to me?” he cried. He walked forward and shook his mother by her shoulders, “WHAT ARE YOU SAYING TO ME?” he growled, with his teeth clenched.

Mrs Wedu whimpered, “We’re not your biological parents, son.”

"WHY ARE YOU SAYING THIS TO ME?" Treasure shouted, tears pouring down his face like rain showers.

"Your mother," Mrs Wedu said, "she was a young, unknown Shanqella woman… You were very, very sick and she didn't want to see you die… she left you with Professor Pittman."

Treasure's heart was beating even faster, "Professor Pittman?"

Mrs Wedu nodded, "She worked at the clinic, it was the worst of times, like today, babies were dying and the mothers were losing their children… she left you in Professor Pittman's arms and told her to look after you… The woman then ran away. And about a month later, the war got worse and on the 7th of April 1966, Professor Pittman had to pack her bags and leave. She had to return to the United States with a shattered heart, but her heart was always with the little boy, YOU. She came back for you, Treasure." Words flew from her mouth that she never thought she'd even think, let alone say out loud. She told him everything that happened.

Treasure's temper blew hot and he started thumping the table with his fist, "Where is she…? My real mother… where is she now?" he barked bearing his teeth.

Mrs Wedu gulped, "She died. She hung herself from the African Juniper tree, the one at the riverbank… When Professor Pittman had to leave, she left me to take care of you. You're like a son to me."

Treasure shook his head, "But, I'm not," he said. "You're just a woman who felt sorry for me and you know," he said and stood up straight and stared in her eyes, "that's the exact tree we call the Chamber. That's where I bring everyone together and try to change what is happening. That's where I try to give hope to every one person who grew up without a mother or a father… I guess… I guess that's where all my hope was lost. Maybe all of this was just meaningless. There is no hope…"

Mrs Wedu gulped, "I'm sorry, son," she croaked. "I've always wanted to tell you, but I couldn't, I just couldn't do it, because I thought you'd leave me."

Treasure yanked his backpack with his Video Camera, "Well, you've lost me for good," he stormed out of the house.

Mrs Wedu shouted his name running after him, crying but Treasure ran as fast as he could and only rested beneath the African Juniper tree at the riverbank. He leapt over, panting, weeping and he screamed. The scream told of the pain within, the confusion. He craved the comfort of his mother, his real mother. It was the purest way and the only way his soul could ask for help from his mother. There is a cry that a mother can ignore, but there is a cry that will have a mother drop everything in her hands and leap to her child's rescue… That was it. Treasure fainted next to the tree and slept like he never had before.

16

Treasure grunted, tossed and turned. He was dreaming in the early hours of the morning. In the dream, he was sitting in a field of green wheat, the stalks bending lazily in the wind and he was wandering around and marvelling at the grains. In the dream, he was a young boy and ahead of him, was a woman, a beautiful dark skinned woman, with her head covered, wearing a floral habesha dress. She looked just like him, she had his dimples, she was young, she was smiling and she was beckoning him, saying, "Don't be afraid son," in Amharic. She summoned him, "I want to show you something, come."

Treasure ran after her, racing her to the hilltop, up to a precipice with a heavenly view and they stopped. "Look," she said in Amharic, pointing down. It was the whole of Sululta, only different. Everything was green, growing and alive. The cattle were fat, the sheep were white, the kids were playing and laughing, there was no sick child, all of them were happy. He smiled looking down at the green pastures and when he turned aside to look, the woman was walking away. She turned around once more, "I'm your mother," she said. "Don't be afraid, go, I've been watching you." And then she disappeared.

He shouted for her, but she was gone. Simone woke him up, shaking his body and shouting his name repeatedly, "Treasure, Treasure…" He flinched and jumped, with wide-open eyes, sweating, looking around and panicking, "Where am I?" he squeaked.

"It's me, Simone," she said.

"Simone?" he said wide-eyed.

She nodded, "Why did you sleep here?"

Treasure brooded and did not want to tell her. He remembered the dream vividly.

"You were calling out for your mother," Simone said, "in your dream."

Treasure stood up and placed his backpack on his shoulders, "C'mon," he said. "We have a long way to go…"

They began their journey. It was dark and Simone jumped at every noise she heard. The night snakes slithered through the leaves, the owls were hooting and the hyenas laughed. "Treasure!" Simone called in a soft tone.

"What?" he retorted, quite exasperated but kept on walking slowly. She was behind him.

"Treasure!" she shouted again softly.

"What, Simone? I'm right here."

She swallowed, "I'm scared," she murmured and her eyes were glassy. The fear suffocated her like a pillow over her mouth and nose.

Treasure felt his heart sink, he could see in her eyes that she really was scared. He stretched his hand out to her, "C'mon, hold my hand."

Simone clenched Treasure's hand and hooked onto his arm as tight as she could and it helped, she felt a little safer in his arms. They walked in the darker hours of the morning, until it was dawn.

The morning was a bit different. The clouds floated in the morning sky, kissed into brilliant white by the veiled sun. Though they were mostly white, there was a hint of greyness. They were not even half way to their destination.

The walked on for a couple more kilometres. Simone was kind of bored with Treasure's silence, she wandered around, kicking stones, picking them up, humming and at times singing. The clouds above them became denser, casting the meadows into a shadowy grey.

Simone cast her head up, "It's going to rain," she said.

Treasure looked up, "It always does this and then it doesn't."

Simone brooded, scanning the clouds thoroughly, "Nope, this time… it will."

"IT WON'T RAIN," Treasure commanded spelling out the words, annoyed and pestered. She was getting on his nerves. He was tired, hurt and all he wanted was silence.

Simone smiled, shook her head, "Your lack of faith is not going to take us anywhere, you know. Why are we doing all of this if you don't believe it will rain?"

Treasure glanced down at her and kept walking. He began to walk even faster so she would get too tired to talk. Could she please shut up? "I didn't know you talk so much," Treasure murmured.

Simone ignored him and threw her head to the sky again and exhaled, "There's only one problem," she said.

Treasure rolled his eyes skyward, "And what's that?"

"Mosquitoes," she said in a soft tone. "They thrive in water. The mosquito larvae are aquatic, they need a source of standing water that will remain until they are ready to emerge as adults. So if it rains, it will cause an outbreak of more mosquitoes and spreading of the Zika virus, Chikungunya virus, West Nile virus, Malaria and Dengue fever."

Treasure exhaled through tightly pressed lips, "Okay," he retorted absent and kept walking.

Simone rolled her eyes, "Just saying," she said.

"Well, I wish you could really say less now," Treasure growled.

She stuck her tongue out at him, tottering behind him, tired, hungry and thirsty, "Can't we wait here on the road for a lift?" she asked.

"NO," Treasure replied. "We need to keep walking, we don't have much time."

They walked on for a couple more kilometres and then there was a rumble. A convoy of military vehicles were approaching them. Gunshots were fired in the sky and a hand grenade was tossed towards them. "C'mon!" Treasure shouted and they began to run as fast as they could. "Behind that tree, C'mon."

Treasure ran a couple of steps and noticed that Simone was too slow. She had no strength, so he ran back, threw her onto his back, ran towards a tree and they jumped of a ridge, rolled down, hitting their bodies on hard rocks, tumbling in the air. Treasure hit his head, creating an open wound. They landed into a deep chasm.

The military vehicles followed them and surrounded the area into which they had jumped. Scratching and skidding tyres on the hard soil scared them, the soldiers fired rounds of gunshots into the air. They were dressed as pirates and had AK-47 rifles strapped around themselves. They smelt of burnt flesh from the village that they had just invaded. They also smelt of smoke and cheap vodka.

Treasure and Simone hid themselves against the walls of the chasm, breathing heavily, grunting in pain, their bodies were bloody, dry and dusty. Poor Simone had a burst lip and the distinct iron taste of blood was apparent, as though she had just pulled a tooth. Treasure shushed Simone when she whimpered in pain, trying to keep her quiet, "They will kill us if they find us," he said, eyes wide.

A line of soldiers stood at the chasm looking down. It was a deep chasm after all, a long way down. One soldier chuckled conceitedly, "I think I got them!"

The other chuckled conceitedly too, "I got them, I shot first at them."

"Maybe they're not dead," the Commander said. He was wearing shades, his skin was dark and glowing and he had a joint of weed in his mouth. If they're not dead… you'll die in their place… go down there and see if they're dead."

The soldier whimpered, it was really a long way down, "Commander, there is no way they could have survived that fall."

The Commander snatched the man by the throat, "Who's the Commander?" he hissed, tight-jawed and scowling.

"Y-you, you, Commander, Sir," the soldier said, stuttering.

"Then stop being a coward, go down and finish your business."

The soldier swallowed, "Yes, Sir," he said in a softer trembling tone. His heart rate pulsated. It was easy to fall and besides falling, there could be snakes amongst the rocks.

The soldier started to move further down a step. Then there was a call through the walk and talk radio. They were called to Sululta.

"C'mon," the Commander said. "The omens are with you."

The soldier walked back up, relieved. And when Treasure and Simone heard the cars rumbling away, they peered upwards and saw that they were gone. But they were hurt and how were they going to climb back up.

"Did you hear what they said?" Simone asked, trembling. "They're going to Sululta."

Treasure gulped and nodded. He thought of his mother, Lucky and all the kids that they had gathered. The soldiers were going to kill them. He glanced up and around, then heard what sounded like a couple of hyenas laughing. They didn't sound very far off.

Simone breathed heavily, "How do we get out of here?" she said, her voice shaky and panicky. Her knees were shaking. They were both badly injured, Simone had sprained her ankle badly and her arm felt broken. Treasure hurt his ribs falling against the rocks and he couldn't even keep his body upright. How were they going to get out of that chasm?

Treasure quickly rifled through his backpack. The video camera was broken into tiny fragments. He was set ablaze, pulling each piece out of the bag. He felt an arrow pierce his chest, "No, no c'mon, no," he panicked, trying to put the pieces together but they were too severely damaged. He slammed them on the ground in a huge grunt and shouted, clenching his fists and jaw, opening his mouth, with veins exploding from his neck, while his eyes turned as red as fire.

Simone gulped, felt a lump in her throat and she too began to cry. She tried to touch him by his shoulder but Treasure jumped away, "DON'T TOUCH ME, don't you dare say anything to me!" he cried.

She dropped her arm, looked down, picked up the envelope and shook it next to her ear; the tape was also cracked as she heard loose pieces. She didn't tell him and stuck the envelope into her little bag.

Treasure looked around, there was no way out, other than the way they came down. If they walked further, the hyenas wouldn't give them an opportunity to escape. How was he going to get both of them up there? Simone couldn't walk and how would he carry her? They were running out of time.

17

The heavy clouds gathered above them. Treasure unwrapped his jacket around his waist. “I’m gonna have to carry you on my back,” he said.

Simone frowned and thought it was impossible, “You won’t be able to carry both of us-”

“SHUT UP, OKAY!” Treasure snapped at her. “Do you have a better idea? Stop being such a smart mouth and just listen to me, for once.”

He had never spoken to her in that manner and almost felt regret immediately after he snapped at her.

But even through that, Simone never lost her gentle demeanour; she responded with a soft, “Okay.”

She climbed onto his back like a little baby.

“I won’t be able to hold you,” Treasure said. “So hold on tight.”

Treasure tied the jacket around her for extra support. He reached out, fumbled and sometimes fell flat on his face. Simone cried seeing the pain he was bearing, she sank her face into his back as she didn't want to see the moment his body failed and they tumbled back down. Treasure paddled, straddled, crawled, grunted, some of his nails broke completely off his fingers as he grabbed onto those rocks. All he continued saying to himself was, "No pain, no pain, no pain," as he grunted louder and louder, until they reached the top.

When he reached the top, he simply collapsed onto his side and Simone wailed thinking that they were falling down the chasm again. Treasure yanked her hands off her eyes, "We made it!" he said, panting.

She couldn't believe her eyes and she wrapped her arms around him in a tight bear hug. She couldn't resist crying, expressing her thanks and soon the rain began to drop onto them. The clouds where thick and dark above them as loud thunder cracked the air, as if the very heavens might split apart. It poured as though the angels themselves were weeping from heaven.

Treasure took off his jacket, summoned Simone to sit down with her back against his legs and threw the jacket over her head, shielding her like an umbrella.

"What about you?" Simone said.

Treasure looked up, "I'll be fine." The hailstones were hitting hard against him and one large one hit him so severely on his head that it cut him. The blood dripped down his arm, but he kept shielding Simone, making sure nothing landed on her. The stones flew down like bullets and the sky became more and more dark.

The wind blew fiercer and the hailstones subsided. However, it became worse as the earthy smell permeated and from a distance, grey showers were lifted by a strong wind, heading directly towards them… it was a hurricane. The rain soaked the tin rooves a distance away, the thunder rumbled and the wind blew ferociously.

"TREASURE," Simone shouted. "It's a hurricane."

Treasure's eyes resembled marbles, "Yeah, we need to get away from here."

He trembled looking around for shelter. What was he going to do? They would never survive that. How was he going to carry Simone? The storm was getting closer. There were some huge rocks across from them, stacked on top of one another that seemed like a little cave. "There," Treasure shouted. "We need to reach for that place… can you make it?"

Simone gulped and looked at her ankle, which was swollen and blue. She wanted to ignore the pain on her foot. "I can try," she said.

Treasure shook his head, "I'll pick you up again… C'mon," he lifted her up in his arms and she hoisted herself onto his back, like a little baby, as he ran towards the entrance. She bounced on his back, looking backwards. The storm was right behind them, showering down. The wind blew Treasure ferociously, but could not toss him back and forth, because Simone strengthened his weight.

Simone winced and closed her eyes. Treasure ran, grunting. He'd never seen so much rain in his life. He ran until he reached the cave, placed Simone gently down, panting, "We're safe now," he said, winded. He took his jacket and laid it on the ground for her to sit, "Here, sit on this."

The storm was fierce and unfriendly and back home, the soldiers were invading the houses, crashing into straw huts with vans, trampling on people with tyres. The women wailed, the children screamed, all running in the vicious storm.

The tree that Treasure and Simone had sat beneath was uprooted by the wind and blown away, cows rolled with the wind, mooing. They would have never made it.

Treasure embraced her, covering her up with his arms, making her as comfortable and painless as he could. She was shaking and cold, crying. She stared at him, why can one boy go through so much trouble? She looked at his bruised, swollen and cut knuckles and she massaged them gently with her thumb, looking at him in his eyes, "I'm sorry," she muttered in a sincerely comforting manner.

Treasure looked down at her, "It's not your fault."

She paused, staring at him, her heart swelled, "I wish I could take the pain away," she said.

Treasure wished the pain wasn't even there. He gulped without a response and they watched the storm raging passed. This was going to destroy a lot of things. The clinical tents, the food garden that they started, "Everything is going to be ruined," Treasure said. "The food gardens, houses, the clinics… everything is going to be destroyed. Everything we worked for."

Simone stroked his arm, "Don't think about it, alright," she said. "You did everything you could. You're a strong man, Treasure. Nobody can do the things you do. You're smart, intelligent, brave and courageous… Don't give up on us."

Treasure felt a rush of energy he couldn't explain. He looked deep inside her eyes. She was talking from her soul. Her heart echoed his pain, he could see the compassion in her eyes. Their faces moved closer to one another, closer and closer, then their lips touched, soft and cold, as they kissed. And how it happened, neither of them could explain. They stammered and stuttered apologies to each other, embarrassed, unable to look each other in the eyes and it was awkward. Nevertheless, both felt an electric current surging through their bodies and it felt so good. Was it love they felt?

The rain continued unabated and a deep sleep came over them. The whole night, they were wrapped in each other's arms and it rained right through until the next morning. Perhaps it was exactly what was supposed to happen.

18

This day too was different. The sun was shining brightly, the birds were chirping louder and the earth looked cleaner. However, back home, it was a catastrophe. The soldiers demolished all the grass huts and the hurricane destroyed everything man made that stood. Many houses collapsed, many babies and people died. The storm disabled the soldiers from walking freely in the village to do as they pleased, so they had to drive away from it. Less people were killed by the storm, than those killed by the soldiers.

The roof of Treasure's house caved in as though there never was one. Professor Pittman drove to Treasure's house and shouted for Treasure and for Mrs Wedu as she parked her van. Buried beneath the tin of the roof, logs and mud bricks, Mrs Wedu whimpered from beneath, "I'm here," she murmured, muffled. The soldiers didn't get her, but the storm did. In fact anyone who was not struck by the storm, was somehow struck by the soldiers.

Professor Pittman threw the rusted roof tins aside one by one, ripping them off as if they were sheets of paper and pulled Mrs Wedu from beneath them, dragging her out from the collapsed house. She was badly injured, her head was bruised, her leg was cut and the blood had become crusty and dry on her forehead, she grunted and winced in pain as Professor Pittman pulled her out and examined her, "Mrs Wedu, can you tell me what day it is?"

Mrs Wedu mumbled some words that weren't clear.

"I can't hear you, Mrs Wedu."

"Where's Treasure?" Mrs Wedu mumbled.

Professor Pittman's eyes widened, "Oh my God, is he here?" she panicked looking around. "Treasure, Treasure!" she shouted.

Mrs Wedu gestured lifting her hand, "He's not here," she mumbled.

"What?"

"He's not here," she mumbled again and her words were clearer.

"Where is he? Mrs Wedu?"

Mrs Wedu gasped, trying to utter the words but she couldn't get them out, her eyes shut and she stopped breathing. She was dead.

Professor Pittman wailed and cried heavily over her, with her head on her lap, but no one was there.

At this exact time, Treasure woke up, abruptly from his sleep, breathing heavily and grunting, "Something is wrong," he said, "we need to go."

Treasure looked around and panicked again. "Where's the envelope?" he rifled through his bag and threw his hands on his head. "The envelope, I left it down there!" He slapped his forehead with his palms grunting.

Simone pulled out the envelope from her little bag and proffered it to him, "Here it is."

He turned around abruptly. It was like the heavens opened. He leapt to her thanking her and tried to grab the envelope but she ripped it away from his reach and shook her head, "Nope, when you get mad, you throw things away, so I'll keep it."

His eyes beamed and a little lopsided smirk bubbled on his face and he nodded.

Simone grunted squinting her eyes as the sun penetrated them.

"We need to go now," Treasure said. He looked around and flew to a nearby dried tree, broke a branch from the tree for Simone to limp on, ran back and proffered it to her, "Use this, will it help?"

Simone nodded.

"Okay c'mon, quick, we need to go," Treasure said, picking up his jacket and backpack.

They rose and made their way onto the road again. The town of Addis Ababa was already close by. They could see the post office. But even in that town, the hurricane had left a bit of a mess, even though it was not that severe, there was a rush of people and tourists.

They shoved and squeezed through the crowd making their way to the front desk, "Excuse," Treasure shouted at the lady at the front desk. "Excuse me, Ma'am."

The woman was too busy to hear them; there were people in line motioning their letters to her.

Simone paused for a while and shrieked from the depth of her stomach, "SHUT UP!"

The cacophony stopped immediately.

"Can you help us please?" she commanded.

The people saw how messy their clothes and faces were as well as the blood on Treasure's shirt. They gave them space to move forward to the counter, parting aside, one by one.

Treasure pulled out the envelope and proffered it to the lady, "We need to send this letter," he said.

"And where is it going?" the woman retorted with a sullen attitude clearly indicating she was annoyed.

"America, it's going to America."

The patrons looked at each other and there was a short surge of silence. America? The patrons thought. It was unusual for a children so young to send a letters outside of Ethiopia. It was usually to their father's and brother's at the military camp in Ethiopia, never America.

"Well, do you have a hundred birr?"

Treasure gulped then glanced at Simone and back at the lady and shook his head, "No, Ma'am."

Simone pulled Treasure by the arm, frowning, "Wait Treasure, we raised a hundred and eighty birr," she said.

"Ssshh," Treasure whispered, dropping his head lower avoiding eye contact with the front desk lady. "I don't have it."

"Well, do you have it?" the lady said glancing at both of them.

Treasure shook his head, "No Ma'am, but it's important that we send it, so we can end the war and stop the children from dying. The Americans will come and help us and save the children. More doctors will come."

The lady frowned lifted her one brow above the other thinking of the lunacy that she was hearing, she snorted, "The American's…?" she sneered with her gaze dropped. "You kids think I have time for games. Please step out of the line, next," the woman said absently.

The cacophony continued.

"C'mon, let's go," Treasure said and pulled Simone by the arm.

Simone kept asking Treasure what he did with the money, but Treasure kept ignoring her, pulling her by the arm, out of the post office.

She stiffened her body and yanked her arm away, "TREASURE!" she shouted.

Treasure stopped.

"What. Did. You. Do. With. The. Money?" she repeated in a staccato.

"IT'S GONE OKAY!" he snapped. "He stole it all, it-"

"Who?"

"My father," he tossed his hands up, "whoever he is," Treasure said as he sank to his knees and wept. "He took it, all of it… he hit me and he hit mamma, he always hit me… he's not my father," he cried.

Simone stooped next to him and threw her arms over him, "Treasure, I'm so sorry."

"I shouldn't have taken it home," he cried. "I messed up, I messed up everything. Lucky is in jail because of me, I messed up, I really did."

Simone squeezed him tighter, but she didn't know what to say to him anymore. She could feel the pain in her own heart.

Treasure leapt up, unhooked his bag from his shoulders, pulled out his video camera and smashed it on the ground. The pieces scattered everywhere. Simone stood with her hands over her mouth and her eyes wide.

"It's over," he said, crying. "We're going back home."

"And what about the Americans?" Simone squeaked.

"They're not coming, no one is coming, it's over." Treasure took the envelope with the tape inside of it, cast it in the dustbin and walked off with brisk, heavy strides. Simone ran after him crying, she was also limping.

One of the tourists who saw all of this happening, eavesdropped on them, went to the dustbin where Treasure had thrown the envelope and pulled it out.

He read the words written on the outside in pencil.

To the Americans: The babies are dying and we need help immediately.

The address was the same.

FROM: Professor Cathy Pittman

Ethiopia Missions Teamleader

TO:

Carolyn Miles

President & CEO

Save the Children, USA

501 Kings Highway East,

Suite 400

Fairfield,

CT 06825

The tourist was a Jamaican-American man, named Harry Belafonte, an American singer, songwriter, activist and actor and he was visiting Ethiopia. He gazed at Treasure and Simone as they walked away and made his way back towards the post office.

***

TREASURE AND SIMONE got a lift from an old man driving a truck. He was heading to Sululta as well. The man couldn't talk and Simone had to use made up hand signals to talk to him. The old man had no teeth and he waved at everyone he passed.

Treasure didn't say a word all the way home. The whole community was in ruins. Simone swore to herself, that she wouldn't leave his side. She ran with him to his house and he was utterly shocked when he stumbled upon the collapsed house.

He shouted for his mother, lifting up the tins, scanning around.

"Look," Simone said, pointing at the tyre tracks on the floor. "Professor Pittman, she was here. They might be at the clinic."

Treasure and Simone ran as fast as they could. When they got to the clinic, they noticed teenagers who they had trained, running up and down with stretchers. Some were busy reassembling the tents; some of the Hunters were performing CPR on babies.

Lucky was there, helping. Treasure shouted for him and ran to him, they jumped into each other's arms, "I'm glad you're okay," Treasure said and receded. "Where's Professor Pittman… I'm looking for my mother, she wasn't at my house."

He glanced around looking for Professor Pittman. Lucky didn't know what to say and croaked, "Treasure?" he called.

"I have to find Professor Pittman," he said, hastily. "She knows where my mother is."

"Treasure," Lucky said, pulling him on the arms. "Your mother, she's dead."

Treasure's eyes widened and Simone covered her mouth with her hands.

"What are you saying to me?" Treasure said, his voice trembling.

Professor Pittman walked around the corner and her eyes met with Treasure. She could not contain herself, she just cried and Treasure fell onto his knees and wept. Simone and Lucky embraced him, uttering words of comfort.

19

Millions of people perished in the famine and all hope was lost. Hundreds of people and little children were dying.

There were three days of mourning before they laid Mrs Wedu to rest. The women who knew her, scratched their faces, tore out their hair, threw themselves to the ground, fainted and attempted to harm themselves as a manifestation of intense grief.

The sun shone brilliantly and the yellow colour of day beneath its glare was offensively bright and cheerful, although it was a time of sorrow. It was as if the sunrise revealed to Treasure how the world would go on without his mother. Nevertheless, he thought it shouldn't. He wanted everything to be as dark and smoggy as his emotions, he wanted it to be cold and damp with silent air.

However, it was a new day, the birds sang and there were patches of grass sprouting. Treasure, Simone, Lucky and Professor Pittman sat in the front pew and the subdued tears began to flow down their faces. Treasure was not ashamed. He loved her. Nevertheless, she was gone and the light was extinguished forever in his heart, with only memories of her and the love she left in him. He sat in his silent grief and awaited the start of the funeral service.

Even though death was part of everyday life just like war, famine and disease, people took it seriously and personally. Tears still flew steadily, silently down immobile faces. She wasn't the most popular woman, but she was the most respected. Treasure felt bruised inside, numb, empty, walking behind her coffin, saying goodbye although she was gone already. The soul was not willing to acknowledge the finality of death, never to look upon her face again or feel her embrace, see the warmth in her eyes, surrounded and embraced by her love.

A white tent was erected outside Mrs Wedu's house. Her humble abode was shattered. Treasure sat with his hands between his legs and Simone held him by his elbow, she wept more than he did. He watched the coffin lower into the ground, down, down, down and she was laid to rest at her last home, in the soil she once fertilised.

Treasure stood up, to pay his last respects to his mother. He had written a speech and pulled the folded piece of paper out of his pocket. He stared at the paper for a while, brooded and rather thought he should speak from his heart. He crumbled the paper in his hand and shoved it back into his pocket. "I had prepared a speech," he said. "But I'd rather speak from the heart because everything about her is buried there, like the seeds she used to scatter in this garden…"

He stared at her coffin for a while before speaking, he had no more tears to shed, he had already cried her an ocean. "I will always love you mom," he said. "I miss you Imayē, I wish there was a bridge to heaven and those who wanted to visit, could do so freely. I would travel miles and miles just to greet you and see your beautiful smile again. Life without a mother… I don't wish for any child to experience… if there's one thing I could tell every young person out there is: Be grateful and love your mother…you will find no better best friend than your mother in this world. Believe me. She knows you more than anyone does. Respect her, cherish her and love her with all your heart. She's the only one you get, she will be gone one day and you'd find no one like her… when a mother dies, a child's mourning never completely subsides… I have so many 'why's'. She taught me most of the things I know… she taught me everything except… except how to embrace life fully without her… your mother… she's the purest love you'll ever know… You made a promise that you'll only die when I'm strong enough to live without you…" Treasure said and shook his head. "I don't think so, I don't feel any strength, all I feel is pain… I miss you and I love you, Imayē."

Treasure took his seat and there were some sniffs and melancholic silence. The song they sang expressed pensive sadness.

The rain drizzled from heaven and Treasure believed even more, that both of his mothers were watching him. He peered at her garden and there were little green roots sprouting from the ground. The seeds she planted were sprouting. Her faith was not in vain, but life doesn't always work the way we think it should. Sometimes people plant trees they will never shade beneath, plant seeds they would never see growing and raise children they won't have forever, but Mrs Wedu knew one thing, regardless of that, you still need to do what you have to do.

That's what she asked for, to be buried in her garden. The priest cited prayers for her soul and the choir sang to pay their last respects.

Elderly and respected figures sat close to Treasure as the people walked passed to say a few consoling words or a prayer and then left the tent quietly. Treasure wore black clothes that Professor Pittman bought him. He wished it were all over, because most of the people who came to him, didn't even like his mother, they gossiped about her, laughed at her because of her drunk husband, the husband that never even attended her funeral.

***

IT WAS ALL OVER the news, the catastrophe in Ethiopia. It was hell, it was chaos and it was devastating.

'Do they know it's Christmas?' raised £8 million within twelve months of release. The single's worldwide success in raising awareness and financial relief for the victims of the Ethiopian famine led the recording of several other charity singles in the UK and in other countries.

Inspired by the success of the Charity Single, Harry Belafonte sought to record a song with the most famous artists in America and planned to have the proceeds donated to a new organisation called United Support of Artists for Africa (USA for Africa). The non-profit foundation would then feed and relieve starving people in Africa, specifically in Ethiopia, where around one million people died during the country's famine.

Belafonte contacted his fellow fundraiser Ken Kragen, who asked for singers Lionel Richie and Kenny Rogers. "As a father," Belafonte said on the telephone, "it is horrifying to see the harrowing situation I saw in Ethiopia. No child should ever experience what those children are experiencing. With every day that passes, more children and parents are being killed, more innocent childhoods are being smashed to pieces. We need to do something… I found a letter that two teenagers wanted to send to an organisation. They couldn't because they had no money, so they threw the letter away and I took it out of the bin. I wanted to post it, but when I read the outside, it really touched me…" He read from the note, "it said, To the Americans: The babies are dying and we need help immediately… We need to do something Kragen."

Kragen exhaled and felt the pain vicariously, "I will ask some of my clients to participate and I will get back to you. I really believe in it."

"Thanks man, I'd appreciate it," Belafonte said. "I mean, 'Do they know it's Christmas?' raised £8 million within twelve months of release, if they can do it, so can we. All we need to do is to raise the bar. These kids, the teenagers I saw. Their dream is to get the Americans to come help them… Let's give these kids what they want."

Kragen and the two musicians agreed to help with Belafonte's mission and in turn, enlisted the cooperation of Stevie Wonder. They drafted Quincy Jones to co-produce the song and Jones telephoned Michael Jackson for the mission.

The first night of recording the song was the 22nd of January 1985. They worked for weeks and days and called in other artists and on the 28th of January 1985, they held the final night of recording at A&M Recording Studios in Hollywood.

20

June 1985

When local citizens saw the positive outcome of the Young Kings' and Queens' Treasure Hunt programme and the various initiatives to help families rebuild their destroyed homes, and dig wells for the community, everyone, even the women who laughed at Mrs Wedu, became more enthused and ploughed more energy into starting food gardens at their homes. They all came to Treasure for advice every day. It wore him out and he was at his wits end, sometimes he didn't want to talk and all he wanted was to grieve, cry and just let it all out. His mother left him with a message to always help others, regardless of how he feels and if he couldn't, she told him a piece of advice would suffice.

Fewer children began to die as they divided caregiving activities amongst themselves and shared the knowledge that the youngsters taught them. These were young people in control of their destinies. They were rebuilding the fabric of their own communities. They planted food gardens with a variety of foods, rich in nutrients.

The Young Kings and Queens, who were older and in their final year of high school, aimed to ensure that every teenager and child were able to fulfil their potential. As part of their Treasure Hunting programme, they were committed to making sure that every child in Ethiopia was supported to finish school**, every child.**

They wanted a zero dropout rate in schools and pooled together a range of innovative interventions that aimed to eradicate the number of learners who were pushed out of the basic education system before grade 12 each year.

Every day, they went door to door, each one of them, was teaching one, anyone, from children to the elderly. Out of all the people, Simone was a different girl; she broke out of her shell. She had morphed from her cocoon. She inspired young girls in schools to stay in school and not to depend on older men or rich men for money.

Lucky and Simone rolled out another sub-programme they titled YOLO, targeting young people aged 15-24, irrespective of gender.

During the Monday school assembly, Mr Belay, the School Principal, announced that Simone and Treasure had something to share with the scholars and gave them a platform. All the teachers were smiling in awe as Simone stepped forward to the wooden podium and she stood up with sheer confidence in front of the entire school.

The scholars murmured when they saw her moving up to speak. She had never spoken to anyone before. She greeted without a speck of timidity or fear. She was a fearless Queen and the fearless King, Lucky, was standing behind her. The only one missing was the Leading King, Treasure.

"YOLO," she said reading from a paper. "It stands for You Only Live Once. The acronym is very popular amongst us young people. And it means different things to many of us, but mostly, we define it as a pass to do what we want when we want, without considering morality, ethics or the basic teachings of our parents. To put it simply… it invites us to do stupid things."

There were giggles and smiles.

"It was chosen by someone very special to us," she said. "Someone we wish was here with us, someone I look up to, someone who started all of this, someone we need to support and stand with. It resonates strongly with him and us. The YOLO acronym goes with the following tagline: "You only live once, but if you do it right, once is enough… YOLO is aimed at building the resilience among us young people to enable us to withstand the pressures that lead to risk taking. The emphasis is on the developmental needs of the young people that include achieving a sense of identity and a need for positive social interaction; as well as the young person's social skills that include developing our self-confidence, positive self-image, assertiveness and decision-making skills and most importantly, to live our purpose and destiny.

"Our building blocks are," she said and began to count on her fingers, "to seek to build our resilience, self-confidence and self-esteem, reaffirm our human rights in terms of sexual and reproductive health." She was growing all the more enthusiastic as she said these words, "…Minimising new HIV infections among youth through skills development around risky sexual behavior," she continued. "Strengthening knowledge, attitude and skills to voluntarily assume positive practices and sustain positive behavior outcomes…" She paused for a moment and scanned the scholars' faces. They were deadly quiet. They peered attentively at her, with awe.

"Young Kings and Queens," she said finally, "we need to rise up and build the fabric of our own society. We need to stand together, encourage and motivate each other, fight for one another, we will not wait for the state to look after us, we will rise, we will work, we will help and we will strive together as an army." He voice began to tremble and tears welled up in her eyes. "We will stand together, hand in hand, heart to heart and rebuild our society. Young Kings and Queens, WE WILL RISE UP AND BUILD."

Her speech roared over the crowd, followed by a cacophony of applause, cheering, whooping, hollering, clapping and stamping of feet. A palpable excitement buzzed through the charged atmosphere, represented by infectious grins, strangers shaking hands and patting one another on the back. There was a spontaneous outpouring of emotions over the crowd and goose pimples spread across their bodies. The teachers clapped and Professor Pittman was in tears.

***

TREASURE LAY beneath the African Juniper tree, looking up to heaven with his hands tucked behind his head like a pillow. It was quiet with the birds chirping and the river gurgling, a sound he hadn't heard in months. Although it was not much, it was a sign of hope.

He was there because he wished his mother could reappear to him as she did in the dream he had. He wanted to know why she gave up on him. Why did she leave him and kill herself? He had many unanswered questions swarming around his head like bees.

Treasure flinched when he heard the crunching sound of footsteps behind him. Who could it be? It didn't sound like it was one person. He turned around abruptly, wide-eyed and his heart jolted to his throat, making him leap to his feet.

The youngsters marched like a multi-headed beast sharing one brain. Companionship, loyalty and camaraderie oozed in abundance. They paraded like soldiers heading to save a King, holding hands. Lucky and Simone walked in the front. They were all stern with serious expressions. They came to a halt in front of him and Simone stepped forward.

“Simone,” Treasure said, “what’s going on?”

She glanced behind her to the group of youngsters, then back again, “We want you back to lead us,” she said.

Treasure gulped and shook his head, “No, I cannot guys… You guys are better off without me-“

“NO WE’RE NOT,” Lucky retorted from the back and stepped forward. “We all need you, Treasure… You started this remember? You did this for us. If it wasn’t for you, this wouldn’t be happening,” Lucky glanced behind him. “Look at them. They all came out to say thank you… to you and they all want you to lead us.”

There were nods and Treasure scanned their faces noticing the determination radiating from them.

“We cannot do this without you, Young King,” Simone said. “Lead us, you’re the one we want, no one else but you and we will stand by you, all of us-”

“EVEN US!” Kidane blurted from behind and stepped forward with his crew.

Treasure was in awe, then Kidane moved forward to stood in front of Treasure, “We will stand by you too and I'm sorry," Kidane said. "I'm sorry I was such a jerk, I'm sorry for what I did to you guys. I tried to sabotage your dream, but now I want to be part of the dream…"

Kidane picked up one of the stones and beckoned to Lucky to put the stone on his neck. Kidane stooped and Lucky placed the stone on his neck. The crowd was silent and Treasure observed their eyes. He remembered his mother's words of peace and forgiveness. He stepped forward and lifted the stone, the crowd exploded into cheer. Treasure did the same, he bowed, Lucky placed the stone on his neck, Kidane took it off, threw it on the ground and they shook hands. The crowd erupted into a much louder cheer. In their tradition, this was a symbol of peace.

With the cheers came fists in the air and widened eyes. They were electrified, awakened, soaring to new heights of emotion. They picked Treasure up and chanted his name walking up the hill.

He was their hero.

***

THAT EVENING, Treasure returned to his normal duties at Professor Pittman's house. However, this time, he wasn't alone, as Simone and Lucky were with him, on duty that evening, peer educating.

Treasure's spirit was renewed and intact once more. He swore that both his mothers were smiling down upon him from heaven, reasoning that they were together and they were now his guardian angels. He was so happy that he had two, because Simone was kind of a handful for him. The boy had never loved before and he wanted to do it right; she wasn't an open book but he promised to treat her like a Queen and be an example to everyone.

When they reached Professor Pittman's house, they knocked but no one answered, however, the door was open. Treasure beckoned Simone to follow him inside. There was something abnormal about the house. It was emptier. When they reached the dining room, she had everything packed away and there were luggage bags, scattered on the floor.

Treasure frowned, his heart pulsated. Where was Professor Pittman going? He called her name and checked Lelo's room. The child wasn't there, the bed was made up and the room was empty. He shouted once more, running out of the room and stumbled upon Professor Pittman walking out of her room.

"Professor," he said, wide-eyed. "What's going on? Why do you have your bags packed? And where's Lelo?"

Professor Pittman gulped, faking a smile, "They took her," she said in a soft tone.

"Who? Who took her?"

Professor Pittman dragged her suitcase to the dining room without answering. Simone and Treasure looked at each other with concern.

"Professor," Treasure said again, "Who took Lelo?"

Professor Pittman stared at them, with a knot in her throat. "C'mon, have a seat," she said gesturing for them to sit and she sank herself on the couch.

Simone and Treasure sat down slowly, shifting their gaze to the bags on the floor. It was obvious that she was going.

Professor Pittman sighed and smiled tight-lipped, "I'm so proud of you guys," she said sincerely. "So proud of you. I've learnt so much from you Treasure.

And the day your mother left you in my arms, I just knew there was something about you. I always wondered why my heart could never let go of you."

Treasured swallowed and Simone clenched tighter onto his hand.

"But now… now I have to leave you again," she said.

The eyes of Treasure and Simone grew wider, "Why Professor?" they questioned, simultaneously.

She scanned both of them, looking deep into their eyes and a tear rolled down her cheek, "Back home, I have to go back to America and God knows, I don't want to," she cried.

"Then, why are you going, Professor?" Treasure asked.

She pulled out a letter from her bag and extended it to Treasure, "They're dismissing me from all work activities."

Treasure reached for the letter and perused it.

'…I am writing to you about the termination of your employment.

You refused to carry out a lawful and reasonable instruction that was consistent with your contract of employment and in the circumstances, your continued employment during a notice period would be unreasonable. We consider that your actions constitute serious misconduct warranting summary dismissal…'

"But why, Professor?" Treasure blurted.

Professor Pittman smiled at him and told him that she took Lelo to a gastroenterologist concerning the yellowing of her skin and jaundice, which signalled that the liver was under stress and they found an overdose of multivitamins.

"It was me, Professor," Treasure confessed.

Professor Pittman nodded, smiling, "I know-"

"I can go tell them-"

Professor Pittman raised a hand motioning him to stop, shaking her head, "No need to son," she said. "What you did was wrong and she could have died… But, I don't blame you son. You wanted this so badly that you were willing to do anything. I should have been more careful as well, so, I'll take the blame."

“Professor,” Treasure said, his voice trembling and he tried to apologise.

Outside, Professor Pittman’s organisation van pulled in, a man walked out and asked to carry the luggage to the car, to which she assented.

“I do feel guilty about it,” she said. “Sometimes even qualified doctors make a mistake and at times, patients die. But Lelo is alive and well… and so are other children because of you, you saved them, not me.” At this time, she was in tears. “Don’t you dare feel guilty about it. Sometimes you’ll make the wrong decisions and still get to the right place… It was all a learning experience and next time, always asked for help from someone who’s qualified. But I’m still, so so proud of you, both of you.”

They saw into each other’s souls. They hugged and kissed, saying their goodbyes. Their hearts were in their throats. They watched her through the window and she blew a kiss... a single kiss. “I love you,” she said.

Treasure formed a heart with his hand, pointed back at her and they watched the car grow smaller and smaller, until they could not see her any longer. Simone and Treasure held each other, weeping and walked back home.

21

June 1985

Four months after the release of *We are the World,* USA for Africa had taken in almost $10.8 million. The majority of the money came from record sales within the US. Members of the public also donated money—almost $1.3 million within the same time period. In May 1985, USA for Africa officials estimated that they had sold between $45 million and $47 million worth of official merchandise around the world. Organiser Ken Kragen announced that they would not be distributing all of the money at once. Instead, he revealed that the foundation would be looking into finding a long-term solution for Africa's problems. "We could go out and spend it all in one shot. Maybe we'd save some lives in the short-term but it would be like putting a Band-Aid over a serious wound." Kragen noted that experts had predicted that it would take at least 10 to 20 years to make a slight difference to Africa's long-term problems.

Peace reigned throughout Ethiopia. The war had ceased with the help of international humanitarian movements of peace.

The Save the Children organisation setup camps on a huge plot of land, large enough to accommodate all the people who had lost their houses including Lucky who lost his house as well.

Lelo had recovered immensely, her hair had grown back and black again, she was a healthy girl now, running around and playing with other kids. She stood in the garden, watching Treasure and Simone ploughing the soil, while the sun pressed hard onto their skins.

Lelo had a little boy pinned to her back with a rectangular cloth. There was a loud roaring aerodynamic sound coming from the clouds and Lelo was the first to hear it. She looked up, blocked the sun with her hand, shading her eyes and peered into heaven with squinted eyes at the shiny object that moved towards them until she saw what it was. "Treasure," she shouted and pointed to the sky, "Look, an aeroplane."

Treasure and Simone were teaching a group of women how to plough and plant seeds on the hard soil outside at the camp site. They heard a rumbling sound up in the clouds but not only them.

Treasure glanced up in the air, but there were no clouds, so it couldn't be thunder. He saw something shiny a distance away in the air, "Simone," he said, beckoning at her and pointed upwards. "Look, you see that, Lelo is showing us the aeroplane."

Simone looked at Treasure and thought he was becoming crazy, because aeroplanes always flew past their region, almost every day. "They always fly here Treasure," she said, her face doleful.

"I know, but not these ones!" Treasure's face beamed and morphed into a big smile. "They came to save us!"

Simone sighed and felt a lump somewhere in her throat. She thought Treasure was really losing it now. "Treasure please, don't do this," she said her voice shaky. "The Americans are not coming."

Treasure smiled even more broadly with his gaze still focussed on the sky, laughed out loud and dropped the shovel to the ground, "They're here," he said and with a softer shout, "the Americans are here!" The woman ploughing nearby looked at him, people sitting outside their homes heard him and they too thought the boy was crazy. They shook their heads in pity listening to battery-operated radios. Nevertheless, Treasure was relentless and shouted all the more louder. His fist flew to the air and veins popped out of his neck, "They're here, THE AMERICANS, ARE HERE!"

The elders looked at each other but Treasure continued staring up, then he started waving, shouting, dancing and jumping. Simone tried to stop him, but Treasure became more relentless and started jumping. Tears began to pour out of her eyes; her friend had gone mad, she thought.

As Treasure waved in the sky, he saw something drop from the aeroplane and he ran towards it. This had gotten everyone's attention and everyone started standing up when sacks began to land on the dry fields. Treasure ran and ran, stretching his legs to the maximum and dropped onto his knees when he reached the bag. He then began to rip it apart, panting, with saliva dripping from his mouth and his heart beating out of his chest. He fiddled and tore the sack apart and opened it. His eyes went wide, with a broad grin exposing all of his teeth. He yelled and pumped his fist in the air as though he had won a gold medal and pulled out what was in the bag. Treasure leapt onto his feet and lifted two tins of baked beans, shouting to the rest of the members of his community in Amharic, "Food!" he yelled with veins protruding from his neck. "The Americans have brought us food!" he shouted even louder.

The people of the community began to murmur, their expressions turned serious and they began to walk towards Treasure. When they realised it was food that Treasure held in his hands, they all began to beckon one another and began shouting, "The Americans have come to save us!" Everyone yelled and shrieked in excitement.

The first USA for Africa cargo jet carrying food, medicine and clothing departed for Ethiopia and Sudan. It stopped *en route* in New York, where 15 000 t-shirts were added to the cargo. Included in the supplies were high-protein biscuits, high-protein vitamins, medicines, tents, blankets and refrigeration equipment. Harry Belafonte, representing the USA for Africa musicians, visited Sudan in the same month. The trip was his last stop on a four-nation tour of Africa. Tanzanian Prime Minister Salim Ahmed Salim greeted and praised Belafonte, telling him, "I personally and the people of Tanzania are moved by this tremendous example of human solidarity."

There was hope for Africa again.

Professor Pittman was at her favourite coffee shop. She was talking to the woman at the counter, about how beautiful the day was when the news came over the TV pinned to the wall.

She lifted her gaze to the TV and her heart leapt when she saw the headline:

Three Ethiopian youngsters beg for USA to help Africa

"Turn that up!" she shouted at the woman, wide-eyed pointing to the TV set. "Turn that up."

The woman frowned and turned up the TV.

The reporter announced that Harry Belafonte, an American singer, songwriter, activist and actor, found the tape when he visited Ethiopia and it inspired him to bring together all the best singers and record a hit album called, *We are the World.*

The news report featured the video that Treasure had captured. They were sitting beneath the tree, Treasure, Lucky and Simone, with the camera in front of them.

They had their hands clenched tightly together, looking directly at the video camera lens.

Treasure spoke, 'Our brothers and sisters are dying,' he said. 'we need help… we need the doctors to come help us, even if it's an hour, a day, a week, a month… or for a lifetime. We need you to stand with us. We are dying… If the world would get together and unite and give a helping hand… the world will be a better place. We need the Americans to come help us… Just like Professor Pittman. She's saving our lives… and we need more people like her.'

They showed some shots Treasure had taken from the Save the Children clinic showing scrawny little babies, the nurses and doctors scurrying through the tents attending to the babies, children and their mothers, wailing in the background and they showed Professor Pittman, caught up passionately in her duties.

The reporter appeared again on the screen, "And that's our heroin, Professor Pittman a Paediatric Specialist who was actually dismissed from her duties a couple of months ago due to negligence and a near death case of a child. And the whole of America is behind her saying, 'Well done. You are America's hero!'"

They played the song and Professor Pittman wept endearingly, with her hand over her mouth and then she stormed out of the store. Right at the door, she ran into Ralf Krampe, who had come to tell her the news; he had the newspaper in his hand, "Cathy," Ralf blurted. "Did you see the news?"

"Yes, I just saw it," Professor Pittman cried, nodding rapidly, her face damp with tears and she embraced him with a hug that was stronger than anything he'd ever known. Her heart was dancing and her soul was singing. This is exactly what purpose and destiny was. It felt like a self-fulfilling prophecy.

***

MEANWHILE IN SULULTA, the aeroplanes glided in the air, dropping bags filled with nutritious food, sweets and toys. Children laughed and danced. They played the song on more than seven thousand radio stations across the world.

Lucky came running to Treasure shouting and carrying a battery operated radio, "Treasure, you were right!" Lucky said panting and breathless. "The Americans… they're here…" Lucky turned up the radio and hoisted it to Treasure's ear, "Listen, this is for you…"

There comes a time when we heed a certain call
When the world must come together as one
There are people dying
And it's time to lend a hand to life
The greatest gift of all

We can't go on pretending day by day
That someone somewhere will soon make a change
We're all a part of God's great big family
And the truth, you know,
Love is all we need

We are the world,
We are the children
We are the ones who make a brighter day
So, let's start giving
There's a choice we're making
We're saving our own lives
It's true we'll make a better day
Just you and me

Send them your heart so they'll know that someone cares
And their lives will be stronger and free
As God has shown us by turning stone to bread
And so we all must lend a helping hand…'

USA for Africa - Treasure's dream became a reality. Like many other African children, all he needed was a little help from everyone. If people would come together for a common purpose and give a helping hand through their talents and gifts, which are treasures to the world, the world would be a better place.

We are the world, We are the children, We are the ones who make a brighter day, so let's start giving… Shalom.

THE END

ACKNOWLEDGEMENT

Every year, more than seven million children still die before their fifth birthdays, largely due to preventable and treatable causes like pneumonia, diarrhoea and malaria.

This one gesture of people getting together, mobilising their gifts, talents, their inner and outer 'treasures' and aiming towards a bigger purpose, grew throughout the world. It had a cascading effect. They passed it forward for years and it still has impact, until today.

In 2012, Save the Children, started The Every Beat Matters campaign, aimed at ending preventable child deaths.

As part of the campaign, OneRepublic, an American pop rock band, created the recent song 'Feel Again' with the same purpose.

Lead singer Ryan Tedder was inspired to write the song by listening to heartbeats of children in need in remote villages in Malawi and Guatemala. Proceeds from the sale of 'Feel Again' on iTunes will benefit Save the Children, which trained frontline health workers to save children's lives around the world.

In developing countries, community health workers are often the only link to health care for children who live beyond the reach of hospitals and clinics. They can provide a range of proven, lifesaving services including maternal and new-born care, child health and management of chronic and communicable diseases, such as tuberculosis, AIDS and diabetes. Yet, according to the World Health Organisation, there is a global shortage of at least one million frontline health workers.

In November 2014, Geldof announced that he would be forming a further incarnation of Band Aid, to be known as Band Aid 30, to record an updated version of the charity single, with the proceeds going to treat victims of the Ebola virus in West Africa.

The wheat flour distributed to the famine victims was different to the usual cereal they bought at the market. They baked a special bread from it. The local people named the bread after the great artist and it became known as Michael Bread. It was soft and delicious. Everyone knew what Michael Bread was and remembered it for the rest of their lives.

SPECIAL THANK YOU TO ALL

Original source of information is from Wikipedia and other sources in the public domain.

Every child deserve the basics of life. Why not ask your friends and family to donate to YOLO instead.

www.yolo.org.za/donate

We'd love to hear from you.

A little help can go a long way. We all have a purpose and a Treasure within us and we are ALL Treasure Hunters, so make a difference, You only live once, but if you do it right, once is enough my friend. **#YOLO #PassItForward**. "Pass It Forward," The networking of good deeds through gifts and talents. Which means the recipient of the good deed; needs to pass it forward to ten others or an entire community. However, it needs to be a favour where one can use their gifts to change someone or the world.

ABOUT THE AUTHOR

Brian is a serial entrepreneur as well as a motivational speaker, renowned for his uplifting messages about how people can discover their purpose, leap over obstacles and persevere in the face of adversity. Born in South Africa, his message is known for giving hope to the helpless, using his own personal experiences as a compass to change the world.

He is also an inspirational writer with most of his books focusing on issues that affect society and social ills with a focus on youth. He is spearheading a community development programme called **YOLO** (You Only Live Once), based on **youth as agents of behavioural change**.

The YOLO series has currently five published books:

1. *You Only Live Once, just do it*, a personal development book and the core of the YOLO series,

2. *The man I want*, a novel,

3. *We are the world, we are the children*, a novel,

4. *Taking a knee*, a novel, and

5. *Purpose and Destiny,* a personal development book.

THANK YOU

For the **YOLO** series visit: www.yolo.org.za

CPSIA information can be obtained
at www.ICGtesting.com
Printed in the USA
LVHW011008100319
610109LV00001B/106/P

9 781723 893759